MOUNTAINS OF THE MIND

GILLIAN POLACK

SHOOTING STAR

SHOOTING STAR PRESS

First published in Australia in 2018
by Shooting Star Press
PO Box 6813, Charnwood ACT 2615
info@shootingstar.pub
www.shootingstar.pub

ABN 63 158 506 524

A catalogue record for this book is available from the National Library of Australia.

Polack, Gillian.
Mountains of the Mind
ISBN: 978-1-925821-00-0 PRINT
ISBN: 978-1-925821-01-7 EBOOK

Edited by Irma Gold
Cover illustration by Kathleen Jennings

Design & Typesetting by Wolfgang Bylsma

Contents

This one is for Lesley and Griff

Introduction

I have never met Gillian Polack in person, as she lives on the other side of the world, in the opposite hemisphere, roughly twenty-four hours in my future. We come from different cultural roots, and our life choices also differ, but we match in two areas: we write fiction, and we both studied history. No, three: we both write in English.

I don't know if these are significant enough to qualify me for introductory remarks, but after spending these past few weeks with the stories in this collection, I'm going to attempt noting down a few of the many thoughts the stories generated.

Because one thing I can say without reserve, Gillian Polack is a writer who makes me think.

So let's start with the easy stuff.

I mentioned that we both write in English. We all make assumptions as we try to map our perception of order onto the world. When I traveled in Europe as a student, I encountered many people who assumed that all English-speakers were pretty much alike.

Sadly, at home I've come up against the same blithe assumptions, and even when I'm trying to be conscious, I can walk into unexpected walls. For example, I was deeply absorbed in the story, "Mountains of the Mind," when I hit this line:

The anesthetic had left his mouth feeling like a gibber plain.

Typo, I thought, in my typical American ignorance. And, typically, I discovered that I was wrong. The definition is easy enough to find—*a desert surface covered with closely packed, interlocking angular or rounded rock fragments of pebble and cobble size*—but what is the place of this space in Australian culture? Is it known everywhere, or just locally?

In this story, the gibber plain is merely a simile, representing a moment of sensory awareness rather than plot or character importance, but it served to remind me that Australia's cultural complexity does not conveniently map over that of the USA any more than it does that of the UK, or any other nation in the Commonwealth.

Here's another bit, from "Whims of the Gods:"

No prince would ever be able to hold his face up again after being turned into a galah. Australia, you see, is the dregs right now in fairyland. Too much changing of established tradition. It's these bunyips and things.

As it happens, I've come across bunyips in other spec fic work, but the main point here is, even in the narrator's slyly insouciant POV, there's an awareness for the boundaries of culture and myth, and how they inform one another. This is one of the qualities that drew me deeper into the collection.

In her afterword Gillian Polack calls most of the collection vignettes, a literary catch-all that can include short stories, short short stories, flash fiction, character studies, prose poems, sequences, fables, feghoots, and drabbles.

You could make a case for all these types occurring in the following pages—and your examples might not match with mine. The take-away is that Gillian Polack is not afraid to play with form and narrative devices to achieve her goals. The result is unpredictable stories, affording the reader not only entertainment, but the chance to come away from each piece sifting the many layers of meaning.

If there is a single shared characteristic in her storytelling, I'd say it's the internal narrative. She writes fewer scenes, opting for character immersion, the narrative voice slipping in and out of free indirect discourse.

That's not to say that the stories lack scenes. "Passports," for example, is nearly all scene, but its main character, Kristy, is like most of the other main characters in this collection marginalized experientially, mentally, emotionally. Ditto the darkly witty "Impractical Magic."

Complex stories will speak differently to different readers. To me, the connective element through all the stories is the interior landscape of the mind, with all its strange shapes and symbols, and often invisible but relentless boundaries. Of course other readers will perceive the focus orthogonal to my take.

There are fae and demons, history and alternate history, a tour to Louisiana and a visit to another planet as well as glimpses of life then and now in Australia and Europe, but at heart this is an intelligent, often sharply realized, always compassionate exploration of the complexities of the human mind.

Gillian Polack uses the sometimes bewitching, and sometimes horrific, trappings of the fantastic to underscore the invisible boundaries that consciously or unconsciously divide us from each other.

Compare this insouciant clip from "Whims of the Gods":

I'm back on the set now, but not as the heroine. My bribes just didn't last the distance. Glorizel got picked upon for the frog story, in the end, because, the reasoning went, with a name like that she just had to be bad. Actually, her parents had firmly ordered a boy, and wanted to call him Florizel. Since it was one of my pranks that confused the stork, I suppose I was responsible for it all, in a vague, fairylandish sort of a way.

To Emma's tight inner shackles in "Words":

Different people wake in different ways. Emma always woke up in the worst way possible. She would grope for the alarm clock, feeling the spear-head of icy air deaden her brain as her arm slid out of the bedclothes. Gradually she would inch her way towards the shower, knocking over a chair or bumping into a bookcase with astonishing regularity.

Then outward again, to Judith in the delightful "Impractical Magic":

"My little toe is already damned, according to your Christian beliefs," replied Ashmodai. "As is the rest of me."

"I don't have any Christian beliefs," Judith muttered grumpily, "I'm Jewish. And you don't look damned to me, just damned annoying. That was the last of my good coffee." She had recovered from her shock and she was in prime form. "And now that you've come, you can go again."

Being Jewish crops up repeatedly through the stories. This not a collection of Jewish tales, nor is it focused on the Jewish experience, though that is certainly a significant part of the whole. Likewise historical places and times show up, effortlessly evoked, as one might expect of a professional historian who is also a writer.

If I were to name a theme (a concept I argue with, being primarily a visual reader) it would be the tension between alienation and identity. (If that's even a theme.) Gillian Polack writes about the many boundaries we build between ourselves: cultural and social, religious and generational, sexual and gender, emotional. This includes the boundaries we impose on ourselves, when the world leaves us alone—whether we want it to or not.

When I mentioned to a friend I was reading this collection with the daunting intention of writing my first introduction, the friend said, as people offering advice often do, "Oh, that's *easy*. What writer is she like? Just compare them."

I don't find that easy at all. Especially when the writer in question has been reading history as well as fiction, exponentially widening the field of influence, as is obvious here. But if I *had* to compare her work to any other writer, it would be Virginia Woolf.

Time and again, as another piece immersed me deeply into a character's inner landscape, I'd think of Woolf's narrative approach, with all its complexities. As did Woolf, particularly in *Orlando*, Gillian Polack employs the tropes of speculative fiction while commenting on the truths about the human experience. Likewise, I was reminded of another of Woolf's tropes, especially in her remarkable, later work, *The Years*, as I read stories that dipped into the patterns and paradigms of history.

I see Woolf as a foremother to Gillian Polack, though the two women are separated by culture, time, and geography. I can imagine Gillian writing, all on her own, what Woolf once said:

Lock up your libraries if you like; but there is no gate, no lock, no bolt that you can set upon the freedom of my mind.

I invite you to dip into this immensely complex, highly entertaining collection, and come away thinking.

Sherwood Smith
Westminster, California
2018

Part One

Little Boxes

Once upon a time there were gods and goddesses. They romped gleefully round the Mediterranean, handing out gifts and infants with remarkable even-handedness. Occasionally they lost their divine tempers and handed out things that were less pleasant, but no one is perfect, even on the Mediterranean in ancient times. It was a wonderful place. The people were perfect, the climate adorable, yet still the gods left, eventually. Perhaps even gods get tired of big eyes staring in limpid adoration; who knows?

One of them, a particularly minor deity, with a peculiar sense of mischief and a deep dislike of Prometheus, was the only one to give anyone a parting gift. There was a tinge of sadness to it, for the family to which he gave it was blessed with many daughters, none of whom had borne him children, despite his best efforts. He gave them boxes. Rather suspecting the line might die out, he cleverly allowed the gifts to be inheritable by anyone. Only women could use them fully though, and only women with distinct and perhaps rather odd talents. Having a malicious sense of humour, even towards his beloved humans (gods could afford this sort of thing in those days) he quite failed to explain any of it to anyone at all. Only the boxes remained. Oh, yes, and the fake Mount Olympus.

1. A most perplexing paradox

'I do wish people would leave this precognition stuff alone,' Sherry grumbled to her brother. 'It bothers me no end.'

It had been a hard day at school and she had a stack of corrections to do. The maths tests of eleven-year-olds stood piled high on the kitchen table. Hugh had come to visit and stayed to laugh. As a brother he was distinctly unsympathetic.

'You could at least do my corrections for me,' Sherry wheedled.

Hugh took a cursory glance at the bundle of paper. 'I daresay I could manage simple arithmetic,' that accountant admitted. When he actually had a paper in his hand, though, he stopped dead.

'What's this?' His tone was disgusted.

'Oh, they're working on sets today.'

'I don't even know what a set is,' Hugh said in relief. 'Can I help with your paradox instead?'

'This time some bright woman has gone into a trance and expects to come out with a bestseller.'

'And, by chance, she's hit on the right combination and actually reads the bestseller sometime in the future? But she won't remember, so why are you worrying?'

'Guess some more?'

Hugh groaned.

'Don't tell me she's got a photographic memory?'

'You said it,' his sister replied gloomily. 'Why people don't think before they do this sort of thing, I'll never know. A simple prediction—that doesn't upset me too much. Events will arrange themselves more or less, and as long as it is more and not less, no one gives a damn. It's anything that involves creation that scares me.'

'You're just lazy. Why, anyone can write a bestseller in an evening.'

'Fine, but it's a bestseller in twenty-second-century English.'

'How different is it to modern English?'

'Don't even think of asking,' Sherry stated, gloomily. 'I hate paradoxes.'

'I read a history by a science fiction writer the other day, where all sorts of scientific inventions are made because someone's great-niece marries him and tells him the lot...'

'And if that ever happens I'll blame you *personally* for it,' said Sherry, wrathfully. 'It's bad enough now, being the heir of this family with its blasted mania for ridding the Earth of temporal paradox. If someone invents a time machine as well...' her voice petered out. Hugh chuckled and left her to her novel writing.

His thoughts wandered as he meandered home. Maybe he should be honest about not caring for the time continuum. No one else seemed worried about temporal paradox. Maybe because no one else had that lunatic gift Sherry had inherited. He had, himself, inherited his father's knack with practical things, only it hadn't come in a little black box. Dad had literally given Sherry her gift ('Well, my mother gave it to me this way,' he had said, scorning the laws of genetic inheritance) in a black-wrapped box, with an infinity loop to hold the lid down. It was labelled, appropriately, 'To Pandora'. Was it his father who had sorted out the loop and discovered who would want to use it, and given her that appropriate middle name? She had complained bitterly in her adolescence—people either teased her because she was a drunk, or because they'd never heard her middle name before.

'Why am I Sherry Pandora when you get nice, reasonable Hugh Albert?'

Why indeed? Since Dad had also named him there was probably a joke there, too. Only it was such a subtle joke no one had ever got it. Did Sherry ever play around with time as Dad had done? Not yet. In the three years she'd had the gift, too many people had been abusing time, and, unlike Dad, she had a living to earn, too. Just as well.

A novel in a night! He whistled silently and went on home. His wife greeted him absent-mindedly. It was crony night tonight. Sorry (be polite in your mind and it'll never slip out by mistake) it was the Literature Discussion Group. Maybe it'd be a good idea to encourage her to go back to university. Then she'd see what a lot of horrors her friends were. He grimaced. Too much imagination and not one bit of good common sense between the lot of them. Then he brightened—a least there'd be cake for supper.

Barbara knew that he didn't like her friends—though he would have been surprised to find this out. So at dinner he managed to effect a trade that suited them both in return for "keeping out of the way"—she'd bring some cake and a pot of tea out to the shed. Hugh sighed with relief at having got by the sticky minute without having to lie or go red. Really, finding excuses on these Literary Discussion Nights was getting tough, especially when he suspected Barb suspected that what he was doing in the shed was suspicious. He wondered if she suspected he suspected... No, enough of that. Anyway, it meant a full evening clear to do proper work. He got the car out of the garage and lifted up that beautiful roller door which shut the shed off from the garage. He spent the first two hours reassembling everything he'd had to take apart the week before. Storage was a nuisance. If he got anywhere tonight he wouldn't disassemble it, he decided. No way.

Got anywhere? First he had to decide what he was making. He sort of knew. Oh, nothing so precise as a label or a function. There was just a feeling at the back of his mind that things would go together in a certain way. This nut here, that bolt there. For an accountant he was remarkably skilful with his hands, he congratulated himself. So what if he didn't know the name for any of the sprockets and gadgets and thingummybobs he made. After all he was an accountant.

Sherry had been in poor form tonight, he speculated, as his hands fiddled around. Things seemed to work best when his mind wasn't quite all there. Sherry was always useful for this. At least, having been stuck with a sister, he had an amusing one. Tonight she had hardly sworn once in a sentence. For someone under pressure—and he grunted as his spanner slipped—for someone under pressure, she seemed remarkably calm. For Sherry, anyhow. Calmness for Sherry was not a natural state, he decided, as he stood back to admire his handiwork, handling his spanner with cool aplomb, as if posing for a picture, last century. The lass needed to get married.

"The lass" would have agreed with her brother if she had known his thoughts. The problem lay in certain practical obstacles. During a break in the creation of her novel (those tests would just *have* to wait) she was on the phone to her beloved, of whom neither her brother nor mother was aware. The line was bad (of course) and no listener at her end (she fondly hoped) would have been able to make sense of the conversation.

'It's impossible.' No answer.

'How long will it take?' A surprised pause.

'You're *sure*?' And then, glumly, 'Look, let me just finish this piece of work. It's only a week till the school holidays. It'll be easier to get away then. And besides, I've got my professional integ...' A longer pause, and then a worried, 'Oh *dear*. Promise you'll write the blasted novel then. *Promise*.'

Obviously he did, for she sighed in relief and hung up. She pulled large pieces of drawing paper out of the desk, sharpened numerous black lead pencils, searched out erasers, and then sat at the desk, staring at the paper, chewing her nails, and wishing for life to be fair. Every now and then she'd look across at her little black box, thinking, *One day, I'll get you...* in the most threatening tone possible. Of course, she never would. Too much was at stake. While the box existed, it had to be used. And if it were used once (ruefully, she knew this) there was every chance of it being used again, for one reason or another. It was not pure altruism that guided her hand across the paper, though she genuinely enjoyed resolving temporal paradox. Beating science at its own game was something she enjoyed immensely. Picking other people's minds was the other thing she enjoyed—just as her boyfriend enjoyed archival research. Now she was doing both, and her pencil flew over the pages, drawing diagram after diagram.

She had to ring up school and claim illness before she slept a bit (no use working during the day—the other mind was concentrated on the wrong things, then). She wrote in her private diary what was happening (no use creating paradoxes by leaving the future ignorant of the past) and got back to work around dusk.

It was three in the morning before she slipped out of the house. It was a surreptitious movement, at a time when the city was still and terrifying. Her roll of papers was clutched tightly under one arm, and an umbrella with a sharp point in the other. She did not need the latter. It was more for reassurance. She was nervous of the night. So much to hang on so little, at this point. It was less rape she was scared of than of not reaching her destination, or of something going wrong. This was a symptom of nervousness indeed, for Sherry was scared of the Sydney twilight and had never been out alone at three in the morning. The stillness of the night impressed her as she hurried through it, clinging to the fences of houses, and scurrying across roads like a crab seeking a shell.

Finally, she reached her brother's house. Sherry ignored the front door—her sister-in-law would not relish being woken up. Going around to the shed, she saw with relief, that the light was still on. She glanced in the window. The view was a surprise. She wouldn't have known from the diagram that the thing he was building looked so much like its Wellsian counterpart. Anyway, time to move.

'Hugh Albert!' she called out low, and rapped on the window.

He looked up, startled. She waved her papers at him and he motioned for her to go around to the front. Letting her in, he grabbed at the papers in a brotherly way.

'Let's see. Is it the novel? What would you do if I ripped it up?'

Sherry chuckled. 'You'd half kill me,' she said.

'*I'd* half kill *you*...' And Hugh looked at the papers. And kept on looking. Finally a disappointed mutter emerged.

'It wasn't my invention then.' It was as if Doomsday had been heralded.

The lady chuckled again.

'You loon. I used the loop. Only the shape is unoriginal. Jules Verne, I believe.'

Hugh became suspicious. 'So why did you bring the plans here?'

'Because they won't work. I used the loop, didn't I? And I tell you, they won't work. The sprocket here is the wrong one. And I can't find the right one for you.'

Disconsolate, Hugh looked at his oversized toy. 'And I didn't even know what it would do! Ah well, I'd better take it apart if it won't work. I suppose it would've had to come down tomorrow anyway.'

Sherry looked kindly and thoughtful and suggested they wheel it to her place and at least he could come and look at it for a few days. 'Goodness knows, I've got enough space. It's not as if I was overabundantly endowed with possessions.'

Hugh brightened at once and tiptoed indoors to get his coat. While he was getting it, Sherry tinkered carefully with a couple of thingummybobs. When he came back, Hugh wistfully suggested they at least try it out. 'It may save a trip—you're not always right, you know. Besides, it's only ten minutes from being finished.'

His sister perched on a wooden crate and waited patiently for an hour. Finally her brother grunted. 'It's ready.' And he started the build-up. He believed in machines that whispered rather than shouted but just adored machine noises. An important part of tinkering, for him, was the lead-up to the first tryout. A rumble and a bang emerged from his throat, then a stuttering putter-putter as he made connection. The putter-putter revved up to a whizz as he waited for everything to happen. The whizz died away.

Dog-sad eyes looked across the shed. 'You were right.'

They pushed the machine to Sherry's house with a slowness born of desolation rather than the earliness of the hour. Hugh had a cup of coffee in Sherry's kitchen. He was fidgety and aimless, neither wanting to remain nor move. So he had a whisky. And then another. Finally, as dawn was breaking, Sherry pushed him out the door and told him to go home and sleep it off.

Slowly, befuddledly, he agreed.

As soon as he was out of the door, Sherry took the last bolt from her pocket, found a spanner (it was a secret, kept from Hugh for the sake of his morale, that she, too, was mechanically-minded) and fixed the machine. It took a matter of moments. She set the dial and sat in that luxurious armchair her brother had lovingly attached, a large parcel in her lap. A thought struck her. Racing inside she came out with armload after armload of personal possessions until the inside of the machine was filled to bursting point.

Perching on the top of all this, she reached for the switch.

She pulled back quickly. Cursing madly, she raced inside again. She came back with her little black box. Sighing with pleasure, she pulled the lever down with firm finality.

It was at this moment that Hugh returned. 'Hey, Sherry,' he called out, as he ambled in the door, still half drunk. 'I know who you mean. It's like the film, isn't it? That guy with the big jaw. It wasn't Jules Verne at all, it's HG We...'

The words sank into thin air as he saw his sister perched atop his time machine, fading into the future.

2. The Royal Albert

Eventually, Daddy gave up conducting Mummy's symphonies. It wasn't that they were bad. In fact, they won many prizes and even made Mummy some nice royalties. Everyone else performed them, happily. But it just got too embarrassing for Daddy. It was worst, I think, when Daddy used the baton she had lovingly carved him for his fortieth birthday. I remember looking at that baton when I was a child, and being shown the knife she had carved it with, and the black box the knife came in. I've never been allowed to touch that box. I used to think it was just because of the knife, but now I wonder. After all, I'm no longer a child, to cut myself.

My mother is immensely creative. If she hadn't been so creative, in fact, I wouldn't have been born, because her stuff would have been played all along, without that nasty long gap which always depresses them so much. Personally, I don't mind a scrap.

But Mummy always minds everything. She put all her feelings into her compositions, of course, so when Daddy refused to conduct (his orchestra was getting too much for him, he tells me, gloomily) and no one else, she claimed, gave the things any life, well, she pretended to be a housewife. She seethed away over me and my sister in our early childhood.

I was never really brought up as a musician's daughter. I nearly became a muso myself—it was in the blood, I suppose—till I was shown the video that was taken of that famous one performance of Mummy's "Choral Symphony". It achieved a certain notoriety, I suppose. No one talked about it, but everyone knew, I think.

I was surprised how good the symphony was. Of course, I'd never heard Daddy conduct it, only Sergei and he's better with Mahler than Mummy. That explains my ignorance. It has three movements. It's a lovely work, a real laurel on her crown, everyone says. (Music critics have been known to mix metaphors.) Everyone except the police. They may not publicise the evening, but they never take up offers of seats as far as I know, whatever city we end up in. Daddy always sends a few free tickets to the local police station (as a sort of joke, he explained, when he sent me over there with them as a kid), but those seats are always empty. They solved their international murder mysteries that evening and maybe that's all that counts. Men of limited imagination, in the police force.

The tape is really nice. It's also rather funny in places. It was Daddy's first galah (sorry, gala) concert in the Royal Albert Hall, London. If it weren't for the Royal Albert Hall I wouldn't be here. Or, if I were here, I might be a musician. No, I wouldn't really care for that.

The house was full, that night. The camera was artfully set in a loggia box at the side, where of course, everyone could see it. It says a lot for British audiences that they didn't bother staring into it or making silly faces, and only took one glance at the policemen crowding into the box before turning away politely. If I had been there, I would have stared and stared.

The first few minutes were cream pillars and deep red, plush furnishings, and lots of views of the roof, as the gentleman holding the camera took his bearings, worked out where the "on" switch was, and settled down to take a serious film. The section that begins with the audience settling down, and the first violin, singers, and finally Daddy taking bows, has been chopped up. They got rid of all the irrelevant bits. That left mostly Mummy's symphony. I'm so glad they left Daddy's bows in, though. At the beginning, and at the end—gracious bows, acknowledging the audience which was acknowledging a brilliant conductor.

The lights dimmed and the cream in the hall faded. The camera picked up all the red of the boxes opposite and then quickly swivelled back to the orchestra and Daddy. Then it panned the audience, as the strains of the first movement filtered through the air.

A jolt.

Maybe someone had tapped the cameraman on the shoulder, for he quickly moved back to the stage and hesitantly focussed on the soloists. As soon as they were in sharp relief, he dared a close-up. In fact, he needed that close-up.

The soprano's voice was silver-flecked and the alto had one richly tinged with gold and bits of red-brown. As they sang my mother's melody, the silver and gold poured from their mouths and met, twirling and dancing in the air. At the end of each phrase, when the orchestra echoed it, the cluster of glitter would softly float away into the air. The camera stared at this, fascinated, for maybe ten minutes. If the music had not been so lovely, the whole thing would have become very boring.

Another jolt.

The camera bobbed up and down in clumsy acknowledgement and then started to follow one of those baubles as it swam through the room. Behind the music could be heard the muffled arguments of the policemen. Irritating.

As they drifted across the room, those lovely clusters took on a rhythm and a pattern. Happily, in the very order and harmony of the movement, they each selected a different section of the room. By this stage the camera was moving madly from one to the other, and the background voices were pointing out the pattern and attempting to explain it. Finally, an authoritative tone told the camera to focus just on one.

'We have to show this. I don't believe it, and I'm looking at it!'

Sweetly, each twirl of colour was swirling around a chosen person. In a haze of brightness, the sparkle and its human companion would vanish. The audience (except for the policemen, obviously) seemed so intent (or was it yet more politeness?) that they did not notice anything. Mind you, from what I heard of the music in the background, the performance was superb.

The second movement was in A minor. My mother likes horror movies. Unfortunately, she also associates horror movies with A minor.

The movement was desolate, lonesome, and rather macabre. The diligent cameraman caught smiles of diligent masochism on the audience's faces. I began to wish that the man holding that dumb machine would begin to learn from his errors. All his awkward jolting was beginning to jangle my nerves and quite spoiled the concert for me. This time he swung upwards past the orchestra to the topmost layer of the organ pipes. There were big arches like doorways. Oozing black cloud crept though it, trickle by trickle, as the *continuo* reflected the unhappy bass voice. The orchestra strengthened, and the agony of the piece became more acute. The smoke matched it, thickened, became a rich, vile and gloriously nasty well of swelling blackness. Small trickles only reached the audience. Perhaps my mother hid some nice intentions beneath the key and the black depths. She's a nice woman, you know, despite her temper.

The camera followed a bit of the plague-dust. Unfortunately, that telephoto thing (I'm no video whizz) was used throughout.

The vapour chose a person carefully. It made a cloud above their head. The cloud looked rather sweet for a moment, poised above the head like a black aura. It erupted to shower the victim with flecks of venomous dust. His eyes would glaze over as if listening to the music of the underworld. Obviously, the dust turned the performance into something quite other than an ordinary orchestral concert. Then his eyes began to hold so much horror it made me cry out in pain. So many years later, it made me reach out. I raised my hand and was blocked by the hardness of the television screen. I could not prevent his skin ageing.

First it whitened and crinkled, then it became blotched. While the man sat there caught in a trap of fear, more of the ooze swirled around him, in wisps and strands of grey-black. When the movement finished, the body remained. It looked preserved by heat, and by dry conditions.

The final movement was one of relief. Vapours rose from the floor of the auditorium and bathed the listener in a haze of forgetfulness. They obediently gave a standing ovation and filed out of the auditorium.

The camera showed a crowd swarming around my father on the stage as he came out of the wings. The orchestra members and the singers beat the police (but only just) in reprimanding my father. Then it showed Mummy, sitting sagely in his chair, eyes fixed forever on the middle movement.

The police couldn't actually do anything, Mummy claimed, because radiocarbon dating had proven that all the bodies were three thousand years dead. Most never made it to museums, however. Occasionally one turns up, here and there. Sometimes Daddy or Mummy suggests that Daddy playing Mummy's music makes an unbeatable combination. The next day, the then leader of the orchestra sends us a big crate. The one that arrived early one morning when we were in Genoa *really* mystified the landlady. She persisted in thinking Daddy was an archaeologist.

Orchestral pressure accounts for many of the quirks of a conductor.

The Performance

Sheila loved Ibsen. In particular she loved *Ghosts*, one of her favourite plays. Mrs Alving was a strong, brave woman, she visualised, not with the sycophantic strength of Regina, who cared for no one but herself, but with a particularly motherly strength all of her own. That was perhaps why she wanted to play her so very badly. Or maybe it wasn't. Sheila always had trouble understanding her identification with certain characters.

It left her in a haze of uncertainty about herself. Especially as she hadn't wanted to go "onto the stage", as her mother had said, "like a performing seal". It was her father who had suggested that, haphazardly guessing at an attractive career to move her away from her great desire to be an engine driver at age ten. No one was more surprised than that fond parent when the comment was taken seriously, and permanently.

The idea appealed to her, so when an amateur company was auditioning for *Ghosts* some years later, she settled it simply. She had missed the part of Mrs Alving at age fifteen, but Regina wasn't bad for a total beginner. There was talent there, hidden behind the looks and the shuffling helplessness.

Her life was never definite. Always she slid through it vaguely, almost absent-mindedly. She established a fairly solid career for herself, almost despite herself, had a group of friends, none very close. She lacked charm except on stage, and seldom acted a part she disliked.

Sheila often reflected to herself that she was the only good-looking woman of her acquaintance who seldom got a second invitation. By the time she was Mrs Alving's age, she still hadn't married. Her sense of humour and her abstraction kept her from worrying too much.

That is not to say she didn't worry at all. In fact, worry came upon her like a blanket whenever she landed a serious part. Her life came up before her—she herself was on the stage and in the audience, passing for judgement before herself, the critic. She often found herself playing in two performances at once, as Lavarcham or Linda Loman, and as herself. Sheila questioned herself then, with unwonted sharpness, wondering whether abstraction and divorce from daily life couldn't be too great. *Ghosts*, her first and most favourite, always caused the most soul searches.

She questioned herself then… No, that's not right. She pulled herself up sharply. She was Mrs Alving, not Sheila Huntingdale—don't play Sheila, play a definite character, who is marching through life firmly, sacrificing all to give an errant son a chance.

Sounds noble, anyway. Put a bit more vigour into it, that's right, argue against the cleric's objections to your reading material, then defer gracefully to his narrow opinions. You must give the impression of a strong woman confined within the limits of a society that won't let her think independently.

Sheila wished she were like that. If only the limitations were those of the society. Hers were within herself. She had looks, background, education and talent, and now what was she? An actress who barely made enough to live, no secure family life, no children. Anyway, what would be the use of a secure family life? She hated housework. Better to marry someone rich and employ a maid. Some hope!

'Off-prompt, off-prompt,' someone was whispering nearby her. She realised where she was and moved off-prompt. The first step was clumsy, true-life Sheila, but the next step was Mrs Alving—at least she hadn't forgotten to keep talking this time.

It comes to a stage where the words present themselves automatically to the audience, and most times the action continues. Perhaps the worst worry of her life at this time was the sudden realisation of an audience out there, an obscured sea of faces, the front ones staring anonymously, the others blacked out, with the light on her face and the other actors on the stage nearly five hundred miles away.

Then she would have to force herself back onto the stage. Her swimming head would have to be secured and the lights forgotten. The noises off would disappear from her conscious mind, and the play would start to live. It had been easier this time. She had been obsessed with the part of Mrs Alving for so long that only a moment passed before the words, the place and the mood came back to her.

She concentrated on intense pleasure at her son's arrival into the room. What does mother-love really feel like? Is it so gushing, as affective as I make it? Is it tender, or more matter-of-fact? She made it feel as natural as possible, being at least a little thankful that Ibsen couldn't really have known what it was either. Unless father-love was the same as mother-love? Did Ibsen have children? A lot of actors scorned her lack of research. As many scorned her ineptitude offstage. Few scorned her ability.

Perhaps Mrs Alving was as insecure as Sheila. Perhaps that was why she was gushing over Osvald. Sheila tried to put a little of that in, and noticed that it put off the other actors. They were near the end of the season and had relaxed into certain moulds—it was too late to introduce anything new. She reversed to enthusiasm and subdued into quiet attentiveness as she played the helpless female listening to the men talk, then moved into an assertive role again, defending her son to the pastor.

This is what she liked, the interpretation, the change of mood. She herself was phlegmatic. Mood-changing happened best on stage and in character. But it hadn't always. A whole crowd of friends had once been amused, entertained, and finally alienated by her frequent "performances" and changes of character from day to day, moment to moment.

She had been unpredictable and charismatic then, but now she preferred to limit her acting to a professional situation. It wasn't a search for identity or anything like that; that sort of idea was rubbish anyway. It was simply a growing tiredness, laziness, and a wish to take a break and lapse into forgetfulness.

She lapsed into forgetfulness on stage too often now, she thought to herself ruefully, and again took up the part of Mrs Alving, finding place and temper simultaneously. She controlled her voice as she explained to Manders the hold she had over all her life except her husband.

As she described Mrs Alving's uneasy conscience she felt briefly that, on that score, she herself was free from worry.

Sheila planed the next few seconds carefully, building tension and worry deliberately with a little more inflexion than normal, then made an unsteady exit, using the pastor's arm as more of a support than she needed.

She concentrated on the rest of the play closely, even playing Mrs Alving when there was no real need, building up the part, forgetting herself. She had lapsed into real reflection far too much already.

It was bad technique, and showed she was ageing. It detracted from her performance and her sense of her own ability. So she forced Mrs Alving into reality with an effort that surprised her by its necessity.

Then a phrase struck Sheila forcibly—"joy of life". 'Is there salvation in that?' Well, if there was, she had missed out on it. The only joy in life she had known was second-hand, or nearly so.

She remembered sitting alone on a spring day, the sun cool and bright, hummed softly beneath the titter of birds. But that was all. Joy was something she played, not something tangible to be felt within oneself. Sheila suddenly felt overwhelmed with intellectual and emotional stagnation, living as she did as a parasite on other peoples' work.

There was nothing creative, nothing original, about what she did. The emptiness in her life acted as a pool, a mirror, to reflect the emptiness of Mrs Alving's existence to an enthralled audience.

The thread of thought continued throughout the play. Sheila consciously examined the hollowness, the mistakes of her own life to give depth to the character she was portraying.

In the last analysis, the only way she could avoid wandering and her mind meandering away from the stage was to connect her life so closely to her character that there was no escape from either.

And when the play reached its conclusion, the agony of decision which the firm, dutiful, strong-hearted Mrs Alving went through, wasn't so inappropriate for Sheila either.

After the play, she went through the ritual of removing makeup and costume with an uplift of relief. It was firm territory. Agonising decisions could be left alone. Unusually, she headed towards a café, and sat down silently, avoiding the groups of habitual late-night coffee drinkers.

Coffee after coffee was sipped to the dregs as she soothed her mangled thoughts, slowly, deliberately, in a vague order.

The decision was not made in a moment, nor was the idea for it recognised quickly. Life was not a play. Her train of thought would have been barely discernible to any writer with a peephole into her mind. But it came. When she had left the booth and paid her bill, she knew what she wanted from life.

Not denial, either of the life itself or the theatre. She herself reflected wryly that life was no melodrama. Yet for once she had decided to act in a positive fashion, "meaningfully" was the way she put it to herself.

Still deliberate, still certain of what she wanted to do, Sheila went home, and to bed.

The next morning certainty was lost. In fact, Sheila was a little nervous. Today she should begin. Or should she? Should she wait for something to happen? A momentous event that would mark the change in lifestyle. No. That wouldn't do at all. She laughed aloud at her meagre attempt to procrastinate.

In her free time over the next few days, all she did was tidy up. The stray ends of her life were cleared and sorted, built into a cohesive whole. A spring-cleaning began it, with large numbers of reminiscences and souvenirs flung into the rubbish bin. An enormous phone bill added the final touch.

All the friends who had forgotten her, or who had been forgotten by her, had a date with her—a lunch, or just a cup of tea—pleased enough at her remembering them to forgive anything.

Sheila began to watch people in the street. After a life of acting, of playing other people, she finally began to understand what other people were. Of course, she had known how they looked before, all their mannerisms and physical quirks, but now she was learning how they felt, what made them different to herself.

She found out the very limited nature of her knowledge—plays began to lose their depth and she realised how inadequate she was. In her spare time, she read voraciously.

After a month or so this feeling passed away and was replaced with a calm self-satisfaction, almost a conceit. So she relaxed a little. A morning off, or a lunchtime without a book in front of her, were tiny rewards for the gain in identity.

Then the theatre reasserted itself. She couldn't leave it, though her mind had tried to. Now she had to concentrate on a new part, one she was totally unfamiliar with.

The rest of the cast were unfamiliar to her also, and even the director, so she wasn't able to feel her way around with any great ease.

As the part absorbed her more and more, the pristine order of her household relaxed. Trifles began to accumulate in cupboards and on shelves. The artistic arrangement of her watercolours disappeared in a maze of movie posters, an impulse buy at a sale. Whilst she was learning her lines there wasn't much time for extra reading, so she generously returned her books to the library, giving someone else a chance to educate their minds.

Inevitably, everything else slipped by the wayside, slowly. Gradually her life returned to its previous disorder and randomness. And Sheila didn't even notice it. Her part was different in the new play.

Mrs Alving and her incisive nature had been totally submerged in this new and demanding role that now dominated her life. Sheila never could resist trying to live every role she was allocated.

Whims of the Gods

Decidedly, you ought to come to Fairyland one day. My home is worth a visit. It's much more interesting than you'd give it credit for. The trouble is, all you know of it is twee and sweet. Why, my home can be more spectacular than Hollywood. And at least the effects are for real. Well, mostly they are. Times are bad, you know, and we have to cut costs somewhere. At any rate, we don't run around in little rings carrying garlands, or anything like that. Actually, we're more like IBM. Management practice is old hat, because we used it to get rid of all those incompetent witches who had tenure and ran the show. Now everything is done democratically, and nobody is important for very long. In other words, we quarrel.

Well, come to Fairyland one day. Sit in on our quarrels. Take part if you like, but I warn you, that if you decide your brother is to find a leprechaun and get a pot of gold, you have to provide the gold. That decision was made years ago—we needed to cut costs, you know. Anyway, these days we're mostly in the entertainment business, fairy stories and the like. We do a pretty good job, even if I say so myself. We ought to. We've had lots of practice.

I remember once there was a delightful Prince Charming who had to be turned into a frog. We had no choice in the matter, being just hired help. Those great arbiters of fortune, parents who tell tales, forced us into it. An unenviable position. He had blue eyes that positively glowed and was even moderately intelligent. Most unusual for a prince. And such a shame frogs are stupid.

The upshot was, we argued. What else could we do? No good fairy was allowed in this tale, and we all hate being bad. At least, we don't dislike it for its own sake—evil can be quite fun at times—but because it gets us nowhere. The most we can expect is a black mark on our report books, and a certain typecasting. Once wicked, always wicked. So, few taletellers allow us to reform.

No, being good is much more popular, and being neutral is even better. It allows leeway for individual action. At least that's what we say publicly. It also helps that we avoid the nasty punishments. Have you ever been locked up in a deep mine tunnel for a thousand years? That was my punishment once. It's not my idea of an exotic holiday, I can assure you.

But this prince. Now there was a problem. He had to be turned into a particularly noxious green frog with goggly eyes and not one of us was prepared to do it. Actually, to tell the truth, if I hadn't angled myself a date with him that evening, I might have done it for a laugh, but a romantic evening is a romantic evening and not to be spent with green frogs. I'm a, er, well, I call myself an enchantress, but some have been known to think of me in less polite terms. Either way, I'm no naturalist.

I started the argument, unintentionally, by offering to transfer to the Sleeping Beauty role, and then the next in line (Liriel) volunteered to turn human and play the Princess instead of giving the man goggle-eyes. We all protested at that, because princesses always get such an easy time of it. So Liriel backed down and became a mysterious voice on the wind offering him good advice. Other people had even brighter ideas, some of which were just no good for children. Perhaps we should go into the porno business. If we do, I might move out of Sleeping Beauty—who knows what they'd make of it!

Anyway, the subject on hand remained an extraordinarily nice prince for an extraordinarily long time. It was just no use. None of us wanted to turn him into that horrible, green slimy creature. Even a toad has more character than a frog. Finally we broke the impasse by deciding on a toad, and one with red eyes.

The parent who was trying to tell the story must have been relieved. She had turned all pink and embarrassed at what her kid put down to memory loss. Perhaps she was the same mother who employed us for Jack and the Beanstalk, that time we went on strike. Jack never did escape and the giant couldn't decide what to do with him. The mother told her child to 'Go to sleep, dear, and imagine the rest.' If too many parents did that we'd be out of jobs in no time.

I escaped the frog one, anyway, even if they did haul me ingloriously back from the cast of Sleeping Beauty. I never do get to keep a romantic part for long. Too much mischief.

I'm back on the set now, but not as the heroine. My bribes didn't last the distance. Glorizel got picked for the frog story in the end, because, the reasoning went, with a name like that she just had to be bad. Actually, her parents had firmly ordered a boy, and wanted to call him Florizel. Since it was one of my pranks that confused the stork, I suppose I was responsible for it all, in a vague, Fairylandish sort of a way.

So poor old Glor played the tyrant to that gorgeous-looking prince. She found all sorts of weird and wonderful excuses for threatening shape changes and other dark, deep magic. A bit like me, really. Maybe the stork is getting his revenge on me. He's suffered enough at my hands. It's so much fun to point out the wrong house, or to tell him to come early or late, or to young people who have never even dreamed of him before. At least the lady who was telling the story was having a whale of a time with Glor's threats. This is why people like her and me stay employed. We're very popular with the parents—they never have to think of local colour or conversation or about any of the small stuff. Lots of inventiveness. Mind you, all our compatriots hate our guts. Except for the princes—their arranged marriages tend to be so deadly, they often sneak out for a night on the town. Which means I'd better start getting ready soon. My particular Prince Charming for tonight is a stickler for time, so I'd better not be more than an hour late.

To get on with the story, the mother finally got Glor to change the prince into a frog. Really, the two of them had no consideration. He took so long to turn back afterwards that I sat with him all evening. He looked stunning, but when he opened his mouth all he could do was croak! Some people have no consideration for the private lives of actors.

With the actual transformation there were also problems. The mother didn't stick to the script and very nearly turned him into a galah by mistake. If the kid hadn't been listening, and picked her up on it, the cat would really have been among the pigeons.

Certainly our date would have been cancelled, but that's the least of it.

No prince would ever be able to hold his face up again after being turned into a galah. Australia, you see, is the dregs right now in Fairyland. Too much changing of established tradition. It's these bunyips and things. They pack a lot of punch. We don't know how to deal with them and have to get all sorts of foreign experts in at great expense. Not at all popular here, I can assure you.

After the mess with the galah was sorted (boy, did the prince look funny in the middle of it: one-third man, one-third frog, one-third galah) we got back to business and the story went on as usual. I was in charge of props. You didn't realise there were props in fairy stories? Well, that wasn't very bright of you, now was it?

I made sure the ball went into the pond (and the kid had lousy aim), checked that the breeze never mussed her hair, kept the tadpoles young enough so the princess kissed the right frog, that sort of thing.

That scatty mother was hell-bent on making it tough. First she started the story in spring, then she switched to a lovely autumn day with a pleasant breeze and a ton of falling leaves, then it was midsummer. This was all in a two-day period, mind you. Afterwards I spent days explaining it all to the union reps for the seasons and the four winds at the North Pole. They don't really appreciate that sort of thing, you know.

In between getting the leaves to the right state of decay and checking that the pond wasn't dry or overflowing (depending on which season Mum thought it was) I was supposed to supervise the action.

It seemed okay to me. The girl was petulant and a little silly. What can you expect of an infant who throws balls in the water and invites frogs to dinner? The prince is wasted on such a fool. A prince who can read three languages and croak like a frog, married to a child of thirteen who can't even throw a ball straight! That reminds me, I'd better avoid picking her for the Fairyland annual cricket match. We have to pick teams from people we've worked with and she looks worse than useless. Our top bowler is that guy who always lands the part of the village idiot who stands at the crossroads and gives the wrong advice to the sons who are supposed to fail at any given task in any given tale.

Anyway, eventually the action took a nice lively turn, with the princess refusing to kiss the frog, the father remonstrating (*noblesse oblige*, you know) and the frog stamping out in disgust. Ever seen a frog stamp out in disgust? Well, let's be accurate. A red-eyed toad. Told you toads had character. Shame the story was written for a frog, though, because it made everything all too pat.

The stupid fool fell for the girl, of course. I hate happy endings. Especially when they ruin my dates. I'm not certain (because the prince was not exactly eloquent that evening) but I have a nasty suspicion that he was murmuring sweet nothings about that blonde thirteen-year-old idiot.

Tonight's date will be a bit better, I hope. He has a perverse fondness for wicked stepmothers and we get on very well professionally. Extremely well, in fact. Told you toads had character. He started off with character. It wasn't pumped into him to make a story.

At the Seaside

Julie stared at the sand, distant and broad at the base of the cliff. Her blue eyes were wide with interest. The distant figure was like the man she drew in school yesterday, wafer-thin, and so far away. He walked down the beach, but Julie's attention was distracted by the waves—they made a nice rushing sound.

A movement from the other end of the beach called her gaze back and she watched, again intent, as the two people beelined to each other, their footsteps invisible in the vast distance. She wanted to move! To run! To fly! She scampered off home, winged like a bird, and left the two men together on the beach, their talking hushed out by the waves.

Next day she returned. Holidays were long. Julie looked for the two men, and they came. Today she was already tired—she'd helped her mother do shopping in the morning. She had held the purse, feeling everyone's eyes on her as she strutted down the street proudly. She settled down to watch them. Today she'd watch till *they* went away, to show she was a big girl.

Fascination overtook her as they started making furrows in the sand. Slowly, slowly, a big circle began to appear. She remembered using crayons in school.

Suddenly lying flat seemed terribly dull. Julie raced down the path to help the men draw their huge sand picture. She saw Mr Hinks was one of the men. She liked him; he had big brown eyes that crinkled when he smiled. The crow's feet around his eyes were like the bands on a funny twisty shell she'd had once, and the lines on his face when he smiled were like the ripple marks in the sand at low tide. Julie liked to jump hard on the ripple marks, to kill them. Sometimes the sea helped her, sometimes she played alone.

'Mr Hinks,' she asked, 'can I help?'

The man stopped and frowned. She couldn't see what he was drawing with, but it made lovely big furrows. If he let her, she could jump right inside them and play hidey. She looked into his eyes. That was the best way to get anyone to do something. His eyes, deep blue. Brown, brown, she thought and remembered the eyes of her cat which also changed colour. Then she saw the eyes were cold and distant, and ran off quickly. Mr. Hinks was her friend.

She ran back to the path, climbing up the cliff face, stumbling in her confusion. His eyes had been blue. But she knew they were brown. She lay down in her safe spot, where no one could see her. As the pretty pattern emerged on the beach below, she forgot colours and thought of design. It was like a spider web with a circle—a proper circle—at the middle. She sighed. She wished she could draw circles like that.

As it grew dark she felt hungry and went home. Mummy thought she'd better stay away from the beach the next day, because she'd come back after dark. But what about the patterns? If she told her mother about them would it stop her being angry? Her mother always forgot to be angry when she asked questions.

But Julie forgot to ask because she saw a big moth at the front door. It was beautiful and looked as if it would never get old. *Daddy is getting old*, Julie reflected, *that's why his face is so wrinkled and funny. Mr Hinks's face is getting old too. Is Daddy older when he smiles? I'm not going to get old.*

The next day she was up late, and went to play in the park. There was a dead bird. 'It's dead, it's dead!' she screamed, and ran to get Mother. She bumped into a big person, a stranger. 'It's dead.' She sobbed. The stranger questioned her closely, and seemed upset when she found it was only a bird. 'But it's dead,' Julie repeated, and dragged her to see it. She didn't see strangers or dead birds often, and wanted to make them both last.

The stranger looked at the dead bird then looked at Julie. 'But why does it hurt you, little girl?'

I'm a big girl now, I'm five,' Julie said with justifiable pride.

'But why does it hurt you? Death is natural for creatures who live.' She made Julie look into her eyes—they were blue, deep blue, like Mr Hinks's yesterday, like the flower she put in her vase last week. They were cold and distant, so Julie shook off the warm hand.

'You know Mr Hinks? You look like him.'

The woman stiffened, and Julie ran off laughing. 'I won't tell anyone, it's my secret,' she yelled to the park and the lady.

That night her father woke her up, telling her to put her dressing gown on quickly and come and see the star. A real shooting star! It went so slowly Julie was disappointed, but her father made her wish on it anyway. Julie made three wishes, it was so big, then she went back to bed. The next day she had to stay home because of all the strangers. Mother said they must be tourists, so Julie pretended she was one too, and went right over the house and garden, discussing all she saw with Liza, her big doll.

When she finally returned to the beach, she raced to her special place, remembering the picture, spinning like a top, being a bird blown by the wind. The sea roared mournfully, slowly filling the gaping, burnt-out hole where the sand had fused. Julie wept for the loss of the pattern and went home. The whole beach was ugly now.

Stu's Stew

Stu hummed a tune to himself as he watched the pot on the fire. Orange-red crackles spat out and defied the glowing, dying hearth. When the kettle was too hot to handle, the contents would be just right to drink. There was a constancy in the paradoxes of his life that pleased him.

For a moment he foolishly looked away from the enveloping heat. The mirror shining his face back at him was foreign. It showed him an exterior—the hearth, the gaunt face, the door across the far side of a room that didn't really belong in this world. The door marked a boundary. Two things warmed the insides of the boundary—the kettle and the flames. And the flames were dying.

A sad little tune sprang up from nowhere. A martyr's melody.

Ah, it looked cooked. He stirred it with a ladle, then tipped stew into his mouth. It dribbled down his chin and onto his jacket.

At the end he was going to look like himself. Not the self of the glory-posters, but a man who sat by a dying fire, singing nursery songs. Not a hero: a human.

The room was only lit by candles. They flickered wickedly. *If there were more wood, then the fire would burn steadily and the flickers would not affect me. But for more wood I'd have to go outside: I can't do that.*

Stu suddenly realised that he hated the people who had sent him to this place. He hated the aliens who had welcomed him. He even hated his stew. He wanted out.

I'm alone. It had taken him a long time to realise that. Primitive conditions on a primitive planet. The conditions were so. The planet? Obviously all the scientists had got it wrong—that stuff about being welcomed, and our music and arts coming to life on this planet. Stu wondered if the aliens (who he had never met) were capable of laughter. Specifically, of laughing behind their hands. Whether the whole thing was just a practical joke.

If it isn't a joke, it is melodrama. Not a part of my life, normal or extra-terrestrial. The dribbles down his jacket emphasised his prosaicness. He chuckled. I *don't exist here: it's just a story someone's made up.*

He started singing again. An old, old song. Japanese. With desolate lilting modulations. A cry against the night. 'The way is hard,' it called to the darkening candles. 'Let me through, let me through.' The ice of the night was beginning to seep into the room.

The song had finally upset his equilibrium, caused him to feel bitter and regretful. If the song of another, written hundreds of years, before could imbalance him, maybe a song of his own would reverse that. Something to send back to Earth. A message.

He switched on his recorder in the flickering light.

The ashes devouring the hearth held his gaze as he searched for a melody. The tune he composed did not belong to the West or to the East. It was pure and chromatic. The words came easily. It surprised him, for he was no writer. He abandoned his famous harmonies, and left no notes for orchestration. Not even a plagal cadence, which, suitably, hath a dying fall. Just a single, lyrical melody. Shorter than the sputtering candle-ends.

But before he recorded his famous end-song, he recorded this:

This planet is silver green
The air it sparkles too
What just killed me may kill you
I would watch out too.

Stu's stew

Ingredients:

1 kg beef topside, sliced into strips

3 medium onions, chopped finely
2 tbs vegetable oil
¾ cup tomato paste
3 cardamom pods
5 cloves cinnamon sticks to taste (no more than 3 sticks)
1 or 2 inches fresh ginger root, chopped finely (actual amount to taste)
4 cloves garlic, chopped finely
salt to taste
1 tsp turmeric (ground) or 2 tsps (fresh)
1½ tsp ground cumin
1½ tsp ground coriander
1 tsp Kashmiri chilli powder (can use paprika instead)
1 fresh chilli (green is preferable)
1 tsp garam masala

Method:
Heat oil. Fry onions for a few minutes, and then add garlic, ginger, cinnamon, garlic cloves and cardamom. When onion is cooked through and spices are fragrant, add all remaining spices except garam masala. Take this mixture off the heat and run it through a blender. Return it to the heat and add the tomato paste and salt. Then

add beef. Stir well and add water (to reach your preferred consistency) and garam masala.

Note: The aliens obviously did Stu in, because he insisted on carrying all these strange spices with him wherever he went. Either that, or they hated his singing.

Deus ex Machina

You ask me why we did this. It's so difficult to answer. If I can put it into English, can you translate it? Will your printed text—so careful, so slow—catch my words as I say them? Our writing couldn't catch quiet. Can yours? I don't know. I've forgotten everything I once knew. It has sunk deep inside me, overweighed by sorrow and bewilderment. And you want me to explain. Yet when I finally understand it myself, and my speech trips over itself in the haste and delirium of recognition, will you see it? Or will the words on the page continue at the same slow pace. I'm only telling you this because you're alien to me.

When I listen to you, I hear sonority and stopped time. How could you be expected to know the importance of pace, excitement of tone, or that halts can signify confusion and understanding? They can also signal a sore throat. Your tongues continue always—never hasteful, never halting. So I feel I must point out what you miss. What you must include in your translation. And, while I can, before thought begins, I speak with deliberation. As slowly and as carefully as I hear you speak.

After having said that, I'm stuck. Can't go on. Don't know where to start. You know the facts. Please let me restate them. It will give me a fix. I need to start from *somewhere.*

We bombed the earth. It was a war. Wars are very common where there are human beings. Not that *that* counts for much now we've killed ourselves. Then you turn up—real, live aliens.

How can you understand what this means to us? A *deus ex machina* ten days too late? Three hundred people out of billions saved from radioactive death. *Three hundred out of billions.* In my culture it would have been appreciated, the ultimate irony. Or maybe it wouldn't, at least, not as ironical. None of the people you saved were Russian. Good guy, bad guy stuff. The ultimate victory. Boy, Mr President would have been happy. He started this thing you see. No not really. But we like to think so. It's so easy to lay the blame somewhere. On the scientists who created it. On the politicians who negotiated towards it. On the people who dropped it.

We used to think of a red button. Red is danger, you see. And when the button was pushed, the bomb would drop. BOOM! One bomb. *The* bomb. Not lots of little ones. We knew the world would end, but with one little button you can blame it on one little person. And make that person into an anti-hero, larger than life. Once we had a B-grade movie actor as President. It all fits the pattern. We didn't see the rest of the world then (we saw scientists and heroes and villains) and it doesn't exist now. And because you didn't live through it, maybe you can't see the connections. Or maybe you can. I wish I knew *what* I was talking to. You must understand that I'm talking to myself because I don't know how to address you.

There was a great TV series once. *Shōgun*. Everyone in it was treated with wonderful respect or disdain or whatever. Everyone knew where they belonged in the foreign hierarchy, and behaved accordingly. We don't have that in the West, so I don't know how to spot it in you. Wait a minute. That's not true. We do have differences. But it's so important to be equal where I come from, to have equal rights. I dreamed of meeting all the most famous people. Now all the people I ever wanted to meet are dead. I know I wouldn't've got to meet them anyway. Out of my class. Like in England, when I got sent there for work. You knew you didn't belong. Well, you live and learn.

Sorry for the silence. When I run out of things to say, well, it's as if I have a whole lifetime of words to tell you. And nothing to say. So a lot of it is rubbish, and then you get what feels like a three-minute silence (mourning, it used to be I think, a three-minute silence).

Finding reasons for not understanding you doesn't really help me at all, you know.

If I was talking to a pal I'd maybe talk like this. Maybe not. I wouldn't have to explain as much to him. Not that I'm explaining enough to you now. I should talk to you like I do with kids. Treat you like the child I would've had when I married the girl I was going to meet any day. I used to get teased about that at bars when we all got talking—"the girl you'll meet, we know"—and slapped on the back. I know you think I'm off the subject, but I'm not, really. It's impossible to say anything meaningful before I get to the stage where I don't care what I say. Drunk on words. Blabbermouth Joe, they called me. After my mother died, I did the same thing. Just talked and talked and talked. Maybe talking won't give you answers, but it'll sure help me. But it should give you answers. Just listen where there is no sound.

I read a story about that once, listening to the empty air. It was science fiction. Can't remember who by. Don't suppose I'll ever get to read it again. It was more realistic than this. If ever I write science fiction, I'll probably not write the truth either. Reality and truth don't often coincide. Reality is making the life you live seem bearable. Before all this happened, that consisted of not noticing girls who pretended I didn't exist; pretending to myself I really *wanted* to go out with the boys; telling my sister I remembered Mom saying she loved her. Now reality and truth are so far apart, it takes big lies to make life bearable. Pretending Earth still exists. Looking down on the tall buildings and saying to myself, 'It's quiet because it's Sunday and everyone's at home or in church.' Or, 'It's quiet because I'm so far away.' Not saying to myself, 'I want to go home.' Not blaming anyone. Blaming everyone. The pretences continue forever. I don't even know what truth is. But I do know I can't face it.

Sometimes I think that they all faced it. Three years ago. Ten days before you picked me up, backpack and all. Just before the planes and the rest. Fill in the gaps for yourself. You can guess what happened in the world outside. But in the world inside, in people's minds? I think they saw themselves and died of it. That's one explanation for the apocalypse.

You're the ones who are asking me why. But *you* should know. Far, far more than me. You saw it all happen, and could do nothing. You picked us up and nursed us. God, I still don't want to remember the last few years. Did any of the others tell you we hadn't even worked out it *was* three years till last week? Must've. Why would you be asking me now, otherwise. But I'm rambling again. It's because I don't know what to say. And there's no one listening to me, asking me questions.

What people would want to destroy themselves? Not us. We were dead scared of being killed, right from the beginning. There were books about it, and newspaper articles and scare films. Deep down most of us thought it would never happen, but we were terrified anyway. Some people built shelters, took precautions. I bet they were killed anyway. Humankind had a streak of fatality a mile wide. Oh, sure, we were optimists too. And ignorance counted for a lot. We didn't *want* to kill ourselves. We just didn't think we could. Two world wars we survived. Thousands of years of our own savagery. The Roman soldiers marching into Britain. Napoleon invading Egypt. Hitler. No, not even Hitler means much these days. But for us, once, he epitomised the worst in us. Madness, brutality, death. Most of us didn't *want* it. We weren't suicidal. Everyday life was important, though.

It sounds silly. I saw Earth last year. You let me see Earth. All the buildings still standing, everything still there. Just still. And distant, small.

Your question would have made sense to me standing in the ship, looking down from a great height. But we lacked perspective. We saw our own lives and our friends' lives. It's *damn* hard to explain.

Forget about the bomb, forget about the target. Forget about the dead planet and lost hopes, both yours and ours. All that sounds clichéd anyway, when you just state it, outright.

Forget everything, and let me take you back, for an instant to a little life—a girl. I still don't believe she's gone, but she says so much about Earth, and why we destroyed ourselves. We couldn't see outside ourselves, you see. Not ever. Or at least, not often enough to survive.

Yes, perhaps I should explain. It's difficult. Even after three years, it's difficult. And she didn't deserve to die. Maybe no one did. When I talk about her I may be more connected, more coherent than I've been. When I was hiking, I thought of her a lot. We weren't going steady, but I liked her. You don't need the details. Or maybe you do. One bit, anyway. She hurt me and I had to look at her, closely. The last person on Earth I saw clearly. So I'll be coherent, and maybe a bit bitter. I thought you should know.

Who she was definitely doesn't matter to you. *What* she was does. Inside, she was a tiny child. But when I looked at her she blustered. She was confident. Firm, definite, square-looking and attractive. Only just a lady. Oh, she was young, barely out of her teens, and there was an air of unpolished tomboyishness about her, even though she dressed smartly. Perhaps that was why everyone, even me, forgave her the blistering tongue. I blur the edges in my memory, trying to remember her as she would become, not as she actually was.

She kept on announcing to everyone that she was easy to get along with. I would hide inside my own mind when she said that. It just wasn't true. 'Oh me, I'm easy to get along with, but I don't like Thomas.' She'd say it so clearly it would echo round the room. 'He whines and his voice carries. It just gets on my nerves.' Her accent was crisp and deep, West Coast US of A. Another thing she said was, 'Oh, I know I put my foot in it too, you're not the only one, but...'

After a while we got to know that we had to live life by her rules, or avoid her. Cockiness she hated, and inabilities she didn't have, and a whole range of things that don't matter. She loved lecturing people, advising them. Youth was her greatest charm. All of us wilted under the purgatory of her friendship at some stage. And I grew from love to distrust, then through to admiration. Some people, like me, forgave her what she couldn't help being. All of us protected her, and then she flourished, secure.

There was something inside her that just screamed to be protected. Most humans have it. But hers was loud, wail-long. When she was depressed, her defencelessness dominated a room. You know, when I was hiking I was surprised to realise she just wasn't what she seemed. It's strange, isn't it, that a person apparently so direct should hide a self so tight behind a shell of no words. I think inside she may have been artistic, subdued, and, yes, maybe a little bashful. Really.

There were so many of us like that. Given everyday life was so full of hassles, can you understand that we couldn't see solutions for the threats we created. Me, I stopped and thought when I went hiking. And then I ranked things good or bad, tried to find someone to blame. We should have found a psychologist because perhaps the answer is in the shape of our minds. Or an anthropologist. Perhaps our whole culture was so full of the momentum of confused individuals that we couldn't stop ourselves.

I was trying to show you by explaining to my friend what it meant to be human. Even when we thought we were perfect, we sort of knew we weren't. But there was something within us—a vital force, a soul, an intellect. This made us higher than animals. That's important. Each individual was important, however confused. However unhappy. Even though we killed each other and hated each other and didn't even get on in day-to-day life. When my car ran into another man's car I'd be mad at him yet Hitler (I think I mentioned him before) killed millions and millions of people. We were basically nice, but confused, and millions now seems an awful small number.

You're right to ask me why. It matters to us even if that's not your reason for asking. We thought of mankind as the peak of evolution. We believed in survival of the fittest. There's a kind of logic in that because we destroyed ourselves. I'm not bewildered any more. I'm angry. But it's a peaceful feeling. I never want to argue with anyone again. I don't want to struggle. Living is just enough. That doesn't mean I don't argue, that I don't get angry. I'm just as bad, just as confused, as everyone else.

But can't you see, that's the ultimate irony. You came too late and saved anyone you could. Random selection. Even evolution failed us.

Summer Job

Her eyes blurred. She frowned. This job wasn't so easy. Quickly and surreptitiously she screwed her eyes up to clear her vision. Whatever happened, there were two golden rules—nothing must hold the line up, and the supervisor mustn't catch you out. Her vision refocussed on the passing belt, trying to keep pace with the belt. Sarah slowly caught up through a mad whirl of stamping; innumerable objects mazing the eye and befuddling the movement of the hand. Then she settled down again into some sort of routine, a regular rhythm, the machine belching once for every three times she slammed her tool onto the conveyor belt. Out of the corner of a red-rimmed hazel eye, she watched the supervisor pass. Sarah's body untensed from the sudden relief of Anastasia turning the corner, out of sight. No longer did she need to keep her face from being glazed and bored. She wouldn't be reprimanded for laziness for a while now.

That was ridiculous. As if one worked better, bored, if one looked interested. And to be interested in making plastic toys. What a life! Thank God it was only for a few weeks.

The work was so gruelling that many of the students employed by the factory each year didn't last the first week. Sarah, out of pride, had stuck it out for eight days now and never wanted to enter the place again. It *was* becoming better though. Less nausea at the end of the day, the lonesome midnight train ride wasn't so terrifying and, above all, the first pay packet had come in a deep yellow sachet. The contents of that one sachet would cover next year's uni fees. The satisfaction of banking those notes was enough to make up for quite a lot.

It was easier now than it had been at first, too. The backaches were still there, and the exhaustion. The mind still tripped over itself with fleeting thoughts, attempts to cope with the all-pervasive boredom. But now the tasks seemed less impossible. The speed of the line was not so difficult to coordinate with unskilled hand and eye. They packed fourteen boxes in an hour. One hundred and fifty sets of two to a box. And each one had to be stamped individually, or checked for defects, and then to be adjusted to align with the rest. Each small task, assigned to one person, assumed enormous proportions when the flow of toys was swift and never-ending. Sometimes the big bins down the end were emptied. This gave variety as the toys were changed, and maybe two minutes of babbling conversation, but not often.

Packing was the best. It meant standing up. The seats were too high off the ground and the footrests were in the wrong position—a small cause for complaint except during the breaks, when aching shoulders and necks numbed the brain yet a little more. The backs of these high chairs were small, curved, and surprisingly unsupportive. If it weren't for the encouragement of the regular workers, who often spent their meagre free time rubbing sagging muscles, then not even Sarah and her pride would have lasted the distance. The dull ache would have been too overwhelming, pulling and dragging the spirit down to depression.

And the regular workers were so happy, too! They chatted away (sometimes even in the presence of the supervisor) in half a dozen languages. Sarah was paired with a Greek lady called Maria. She had fine, silky black hair which drifted everywhere and had to be confined in a bright scarf which needed continual retying. Although Maria grumbled about it often, she was evidently proud of it, comparing it to Sarah's own rather earthy-coloured curls with a couple of words of utterly incomprehensible English and a flutter of satisfaction from her eloquent hands.

As the days wore on, Sarah managed to look, if not happy, then at least not suicidal. To finish each day was a sign of success, a measure of staying power.

As the days slowly became weeks, she found she was accepted by the open-handed factory girls, and learnt to communicate in their own special language—half English, half sign. Naturally she knew Maria best, as they always worked opposite each other. Eight hours a day made them familiar with each other's mannerisms, and taught Sarah little tricks and ways of cheating to make the job easier. It also taught her a bit about the background of her companion. She had been in Australia, married, for twelve years. Three children and a husband were her leisure activities, plus keeping their Richmond home immaculate and writing letters home to Greece.

Three kids! thought Sarah, pondering it over and over, in a place which offered so little food for thought. *Three kids! And both parents working full time!*

The baby was only six months old. Reluctantly, Sarah felt her curiosity stimulated and she tried to ask more questions, to find out how such an exhausting and unfulfilling life could possibly be worthwhile. It was no use. The language barrier was too great. Sarah valued Maria's appreciation of the attempt at understanding, without a thought of the patronising attitude adopted by the self-conscious university student. She herself was educated, but she had no facility for language in a country where "ethnics" are supposed to be bilingual.

Maria's eldest son was already supposed to be headed for a good career, perhaps in medicine, Maria had hoped. Sarah saw a photo of him—a dramatic–looking child of ten, temperament shining vividly in the sulky, dark face. Sarah's mental comment was that he was probably badly spoilt. He was passing his subjects at school and was evidently a cause for great pride, not the least because he was male, firstborn, and Australian. It was for him she worked, rather than herself. Sarah only began to understand this when she saw the photo of the baby. To give the children a future in Australia was important.

Anastasia appeared from nowhere like an avenging angel out of a Byzantine mosaic. The placidity of her features was at odds with the high, sharp voice, telling them to work, work, no talk. Innocent Sal thought first that the hurried concentration on the job by Maria was due to the pressure of authority alone, perhaps with a touch of understanding of a country-woman's task. In reality, Maria was probably disgusted that this sweet-looking Macedonian, with brown hair, pale skin, and the worst temper in the factory, could be given so much authority, simply because she understood a little English. The girl was only half-educated!

Christmas was arriving, and the work didn't slow. In fact, there was a concerted effort to get as much done as possible, despite the heat and torpidity. The forty-degree temperature was also considered no excuse for slackening, though the factory was a heat-trap. Despite this, the flurry of present-buying pervaded the atmosphere. One day someone from the far end of the belt handed out chocolates. Sarah felt she had to refuse them, as she was only a casual worker and not part of that tight circle of friends. The next day Maria gave her a Christmas card. So Sarah joined in the festive feel and resolved to do something. She decided to be original. She bought a packet of wrapped sweets and sent them down the conveyor belt one by one. Her gambit was greeted with puzzled laughter. Even the supervisor was amused, and joined in later on that day with her own sweets moving down the line on bits of torn-up paper.

Soon Sarah's time at the factory reached an end; next day work finished for the holidays. The differences in lifestyles of the paired workers were obvious when they discussed the vacation. The holiday season was a lot of work for Maria. It was her main break from the factory as well as a time of festivity. She had spring-cleaning to do, family to see, and all the work for Christmas to complete. Her son celebrated his name-day early in the New Year. And she would be home for once to see that her husband and children ate proper meals. All year she had been forced to prepare two of the daily meals and then to be absent whilst the family ate them. Now she would be home. With the baby. She would have three weeks caring for the baby, watching her tiny daughter grow. Christmas was indeed a happy time.

Sarah was looking forward to the parties she'd had to deny herself till now. She could help her mother a bit with the housekeeping, sure, but her contribution to the household funds would lessen the guilty feeling of taking a real holiday. Term holidays were spent mainly writing essays. Now she had till February, no, till March, to do anything she liked in. Maybe in March she'd try for another job, but that still left her over a month to get rid of the stench of the factory and have a glorious break. Time to cultivate a tan!

During that month, Sarah passed the factory often. It seemed strange to see it without smoke at first. Then just when she had become used to it, the black fumes steamed the skyline again. Sometimes she took a different tram to avoid the scent that brought back the nausea and discomfort of those few weeks. Soon she stopped worrying. In her return to study and full-time thought, she put the whole episode out of her mind.

Once, later on, Maria caught the same tram as her. Maria didn't notice Sarah, she was too busy chatting to the other factory girls who had got on the tram with her. It was probably just as well, Sarah reasoned to herself, nervous and fidgety. The confidence of the university student, always precarious, now disappeared beneath an entirely irrational fear. She was scared of returning to the factory life for good. It was as if, by knowing and recognising a factory worker, she was denying herself a career. Sarah recognised the stupidity of that thought. But she still ignored Maria on the tram.

Words

Different people wake in different ways. Emma always woke up in the worst way possible. She would grope for the alarm clock, feeling the spearhead of icy air deaden her brain as her arm slid out of the bedclothes. Gradually she would inch her way towards the shower, knocking over a chair or bumping into a bookcase with astonishing regularity. She also knew, instinctively, how to find the furniture in the half-light of early morning.

It took a good ten minutes of glowing shower water to get rid of the chill bruise and warm her bones. But afterwards she'd be ready for anything. A good solid breakfast followed, then a quick look at the paper, and a slam of the door in her race to catch her train.

She arrived at work, punctual and organised. Emma didn't bother to check the time. She never bothered with inessentials. She walked quickly down the corridor, her footsteps echoing behind her, entering the office just after her, then lapsing into silence as she settled down to work.

As she picked up the pile of papers, she felt a twinge of unease. Was she starting with the wrong thing? It would ruin her day if that happened, it always did. To reassure herself, she took a quick look at the papers in her hands. As she looked, her hands clenched tightly, crinkling the sheet. She could see row upon row of writing, beautifully spaced, leaving triangles and squares of blank space around it. But it was unreadable Perhaps a foreign language? Emma tried to run through the possible languages it could be, but drew a blank. She couldn't think straight.

Not a name came to her mind. There was no doubt she was thinking about it, but in ideas, not words. Practically, to reassure herself, she cast her eyes around the room, trying to name simple things—a desk, a filing cabinet, a window. Nothing. In her mind none of them had names.

Softly, slowly, Emma sat. Tears trickled down her cheeks. They flowed soundlessly, as quietly and swiftly as her life.

She reached for the phone and dialled at random. The numbers meant nothing. A woman answered and spoke to her, an early morning daze in her voice. Emma pleaded for help with the bemused whine of a puppy seeking succour. The voice grew puzzled, then angry and upset. No help came.

She put her head between her hands, and she sobbed. Unable to speak, she gave up the effort it cost to use ideas and memories. As she sobbed herself dry, her body slumped onto the desk. She tried to shut out the world, retreating into herself in an attempt to start the day again. Gradually she blanked out her mind. Then she forced herself to sit upright, to look as if her life were normal. She rested her head on her hands and just sat there, her mind drawn and emptied with grief and confusion. Unconsciously she focussed her gaze on the door.

Eventually it opened and people came in. She let them talk around her. It was no use trying to talk to them—no one could understand her cries for help. They discussed her and talked at her, trying to break down the barrier. Someone picked up the phone and dialled. Most of the people left. There was an attempt to comfort her, treating her like an infant. She would accept no comfort.

In the end a man came in. A doctor. Recognition flared in her mind briefly before it was snuffed out. He poked and peeked and prodded and talked in a soft voice to people around her. She was gently let out of the room and taken home, her eyes glazed and uncaring. A rug was put around her to stop her shivering and someone made a hot cup of tea. He lay down on the bed and slept.

When she woke up it was evening. She roused gradually, staring at the ceiling, then all round her at the familiar, comfortable room. Lying warm and calm under the bedclothes, she was contented and at peace, not trying to name the world or to alienate herself from it by searching for normality. A friend came in and spoke to her, gently. Emma shook her head, indicating inability to understand. The friend frowned slightly and tried again. After a while the friend realised that Emma could not speak. With this she had to be content. She brought in food. Emma gestured thanks and gratitude.

Later she went to sleep again. Dozing lightly and waking peacefully. Once she even slipped out of bed to find some knitting, ransacking the cupboards and scattering wool and bits of material all over the floor. She sat up in bed, the needles clicking, and a meaningless hum emanating from within her. She was happy, but a sense of distance and unreality moulded her thoughts.

She continued with this for perhaps a week—waited on by friends, distracted and vague—until, one day, her mind was forced into activity again.

Aroused from her half-dream by the sound of crashing, she moved to the kitchen. A friend was throwing plate after plate after plate. One by one. Against the wall. Emma touched Barbara lightly on the shoulder and the friend wailed wordlessly, crying to heaven for words to express her agony. Emma heated some milk and calmed Barbara, soothing and understanding, expressing herself in murmurs and sighs. They now moved in the same world.

Later, stirred by some vague remembrance of her previous life, Emma went to look in the letterbox. A large pile-up of papers was there, and lots of letters. She emptied the box and carried the lot inside, scattering white fragments down the garden path as she went.

Emma grinned gleefully and started sorting the envelopes. First she did it by shape. Then she stacked them, making it look like an office desk. She grimaced at the resemblance and knocked the whole pile over.

With each letter, her gaze became more and more lonesome as she prayed for the meanings of the words to spring from the pages in front of her. Eventually she gave up and left the pile, tidy but totally random, sitting on the table.

Bored with order and with searching for meaning in row upon row of scrawl and print, she had turned to the newspapers. Like a busy child, she ripped out the pictures, the edges torn and ragged, then stuck them to the wall. When the wall above the stove was full, she looked for something else to do. Soon the paper was scattered everywhere. Long thin strips of newsprint covered the floor.

From there she proceeded to make patterns. Imagery meant much more than words, so she spent hours creating and recreating diagrams.

The pain of hunger added to the clamour for her attention, so she started cooking. Everything interesting went into the frying pan, from soya sauce and baked beans to egg, onion and dried spaghetti. She stirred it and swished it and drowned it in water till it boiled over and slurped down to the floor. Emma munched it with a calm satisfaction and went to bed.

Barbara didn't seem so content. Between books and television and telephone, she was up all night, searching for a glimmer of meaning. Searching dully for even one word amongst all those lines, all that talk, just one word that made sense. She sat down at the table once, and tried to write. No messages came out of her pen—only meaningless scrawl.

The morning visitors found her dead. Suicide. She couldn't stand the loneliness of being unable to understand.

It affected Emma closely. No longer could she ignore the illness and play like a child. She saw a bleak reality and was forced to look at herself and ask why she had not seen death as a solution.

But how does one ask questions with no words to ask with? No longer self-contained, no longer simply an, amused child, Emma changed yet again. From a cool and mature woman, she had become an infant, with an infant's heedlessness and joy in life and an adult's concentration span. Now little of either remained, except the concentration span.

She withdrew into herself, living on her memories of faces, of noises, of the warmth of people around her. Her family and its caring re-entered her thoughts. She cut herself off from everything outside. Nothing could pierce her inward reflection.

Then one day it ended. Just like that. As suddenly as she had been without words, so she found them again.

No one was with her at the time. Emma woke as if from a dream. Fumbling for reality. Her awakening was abrupt, stumbling, awkward. And when she had changed her clothes and had a shower, her vision was clear. She saw the mess she had made in the kitchen. The pictures above the stove were the first to go, and the glue scraped off after.

Painstakingly she went through the house, inch by inch returning it to its original tidiness, exorcising the blot from her life by savagely exercising her voice and hands, giving names to everything around her. She swore at things and screamed at anything out of place, letting loose the flood of emotion that had waited so long.

And when people came to check on her they found her as she used to be—courteous, undemanding, efficient, and perhaps a little apologetic. It was almost as if she had never changed. But when she was alone and had a little time for reflection, she realised just what she had lost.

Emma was a part of the rest of the world now. She could not escape again.

Time Is

I have a very clear memory from my early adolescence.

It was December and a Saturday afternoon. In Australia, Saturday afternoon is a time of recreation, and my memory is in the back garden of a friend's place I went to every Saturday. The house was a big subdivided Victorian mansion and we had a series of secret clubs in the dilapidated stables out the back. It was a trek from the coach house to the house—there were two gardens, not one, and it was uphill. There is a block of flats there now. Melbourne gardens are big, and this was over an acre.

I was panting round the curved path, aware of my shortness of breath. My chest was wheezing and betraying the asthma that limited my childhood. I was aware of my fat. My glasses were slipping from my nose with the heat of the sun. I passed the peach tree and couldn't stop. There was an urgency now forgotten that overrode the importance of looking at a beautiful thing. So, in that moment, when I realised, not for the first time, that time is transient, I sent myself a message.

I remember the gist of it. When I was younger, we were always being told that childhood was the happiest time of our lives. My early memories must have felt pretty cliché-ridden if I send messages to myself that are reactions to those clichés. Today in a room on the other side of the world, with snow on the ground outside, I can still feel the heat of the Australian summer oozing down my skin. And in my mind is the haunting recollection of the cliché and of the message. But I have lost the import of the message.

Too many. I have sent myself too many moments to remember and I can't recollect this one properly. The gravel under my feet is clear, and a sense of bitterness. The logical message would have been one of rebellion against childhood, a wish to escape it. But I've always been a romantic, never a rebel. My greatest hero was Peter Pan. And he never grew up.

Perhaps I was just reminding myself that—to revert to the clichés teachers spent most of my school years trying to train me out of—happiness is never unalloyed. It would be nice if that were the message in my private time capsule. Philosophical for a twelve-year-old, perhaps, but it means that the times when I was lightning-dead with loneliness in the schoolyard were not the only ones I experienced.

I was in a minority group, an English-speaking Australian ("native" English they called me) amongst a bilingual people. Not Anglo-Saxon in the days when most 'native' speakers seemed to be. And I was not Christian. Not that I thought of any of this at the time. This is further back in time than the message, and I was less sophisticated. At nine years old, one would hope that cultural isolation would go unremarked. And it did. I had to be told about it when I was twenty, a monument to my continuing romantic naïvety. No, the reasons for my exclusion from the group were obvious. "Fattiparatti" I was called. Most sport was denied me. And worse, I was ahead in classes of the Greek and Italian children I mostly mixed with. It's strange that I never have learned Greek and Italian. Maybe the wounds of childhood go deep. That's why it's reassuring to know that, at the beginning of high school, I may have been fairly happy.

It was the first of many messages to myself, that one in Jane's back yard. I'd hear that memory is best in childhood, decided my childhood was nearly over, so hammered home any moments worth the name. For example, it had been raining one day at school. I must have been fourteen. We were outside the gym, waiting for class. That was a beautiful instant of time. The branch of a tree dipped low and sprinkled the gym's tin roof with a generous libation of water. There was a bird singing nearby. Now it is both far away, and very close. The gym was by the school fence of the school, next to the park. There were all sorts of rumours about that park, which everyone tried very hard to hide from me.

After being hurt in childhood, I have the distinct recollection of being protected in adolescence. I wasn't told when fights would be because (I assume) people knew my hatred of violence. And fights were big social events.

I never had to stand up for myself physically. It was partly because I was a girl, and fat. Perhaps there was no social approval attached to defeating someone like me. But more than that, my tongue could lash out in a way that left bullies defenceless. In return for the friendship of one of the toughest girls in the school, I once spoke up for her. It was enough. But perhaps this memory reflects the romantic in me, and not the reality of my past. Suffice it to say that, in a State school, I remember being unusual, not fitting in.

What added to my isolation in childhood and heightened a precarious and pretentious intellectual position in adolescence, made me exactly at home when I reached university. So I stopped sending myself messages.

It was then I started to remember the moments I had set into my mind. They were moulded there, and, at university, I learned skill in pouring wax into the mould to come out with a perfectly detailed model of these reflections. They lacked colour. They still do. Too much a part of myself, they are affected by time and the changes in myself.

Because I can feel the coarse heat on my bare arms, the headache behind my eyes. Because gravel is crunching under my feel and my calves are tired. Because I have to stop just past the peach tree to take medicine for my asthma (which gives me a chance to look at it after all). Because of all this which I still feel today, I am no more capable of objectivity than I was then.

The forgotten part of the message is crucial. I cannot remember a thing I have been forcing down my own throat for years because, somewhere, deep down, I do not want to. It may be painful. It may be palatable. Or it may simply be unromantic.

But it is far more likely that passing time has played me the very trick I tried so hard to escape that Saturday afternoon. When I recreate a memory, I only see the self I have become. The inevitable thought, the necessary logical conclusion I reached that day is lost. Even the cliché I couched the thought in seems distant. But I remember the jog-trot up the gravel path, even if the original reason for running is a mystery. It is the thoughts that change. The sun is mine, even in midwinter.

Breakaway

People surrounded me, crushing and tugging. I wanted to go home.

My eldest brother was in the home team and I was supposed to be cheering him on. I knew nothing of football then and know less now, but I knew it was important. It was a big game—the biggest, he had boomed pleasantly at me. He belonged to the Factories in his unshapen way, muscular and slow-thinking, as neither my twin nor myself ever did. And he was trying to get out.

Like every twenty-year-old, he had realised the prospects ahead of him long ago. If he stayed and worked steadily in his job, he might be foreman when he was forty-five. That meant the same tasks night in, night out for another twenty-five years. He didn't even have the dubious benefit of a day shift. Ten years earlier he had rejected the scholar's way, studying for HSC and a chance at the Equal Opportunity bonuses.

It was unlikely he'd get one anyway, and he knew it. At our school only twenty-four students had managed to qualify for University full-board scholarships since they were established in 2001. That's twenty-four out of thousands. And most of them had suburban backgrounds, of sorts. All the rest of the Industrial Zone bonuses went to kids in the peripheral areas.

That left sport.

Father had reached the City by sport. It's a magical passport. If you're good enough then it gives you authority and makes you big with reputation and glamour. Father had all of that. He played with a big inner-suburban team for five years, found himself a City wife, then came back to the Factories where he belonged. His reputation was still sufficient for him to be appointed coach to our best team. Coach, at twenty-five! Something like that was worth the gruelling effort, George thought.

Me, I've always thought of Mother, City-bred and unused to factory fumes and the startling sterilised and rather dingy cleanliness that went with them.

Rumour had it that discrimination didn't exist in the City, but no number of laws could prevent it in the Factories. Father had begun on the wage of a sixteen-year-old, and was lucky to get that. Pity and scorn were the only gifts the neighbours ever gave her as we arrived, and wasted her to a shadow. There were seven of us, and we all survived to healthy maturity. A small enough family for our area. Mrs Stella next door had sixteen kids. Our mother was considered lucky. If she had remained in the City, she would've had three kids at most.

Aunt Heddie helped. She'd come when Robert and I were about ten, when Josh was born. Dad used to laugh and joke about it, saying she was converted to Factory life. She never was.

Her husband had left her money in his will. It was a mystery to our whole family. She lived off her capital and imported many of her wants from the periphery. In our world all money was spent as it came in. Every gadget, every gimmick had to be bought.

I practically lived in her house. I ate with her, talked with her, even had cooking lessons from her. It was strange, learning how to cook in a society where everything comes ready-made. In Aunt Heddie's rooms I also learned about art. Inevitably, she taught me how to paint. But she didn't have much to do with George at all. He was irreclaimable, she said. And besides, she was there to help Mother. Why should she do something she didn't enjoy? There was no denying the two didn't get on.

So I was alone at the big match. Mother was ill again, and Father and the others knew their way around and had plunged into the crowd as if it were a life-giving pool. No one even seemed to notice me. I slipped out of the grounds with a faint aura of guilt clinging to me and went home to Aunt Heddie. As always, she welcomed me and I painted peacefully until the raucous thumping next door assured me that the game had finished.

With a sigh, I cleaned my brushes and tidied myself up. 'Is it okay if I leave everything out?'

Aunt Heddie wasn't worried. She was easy to manage. Not like Father.

In the beginning, years ago, I used to come for peace and quiet only. Then I started to learn and so did Robert. We both crossed the corridor every day, greeting and grabbing at the richness that was missing at home. Aunt Heddie taught us that it wasn't our Father's fault, and so we blamed him, in an excusing way, for not becoming Citified during his five years there.

Our rooms were noisy and jubilant. Obviously, George had been given some sort of recognition for his undoubted abilities. I slipped in without being noticed and I drank in the excitement and colour. I didn't remember ever having seen our house so bright and cheerful, not even at Christmas. Dad had lashed out and bought bright fruits from the supermarket, the sort we had always stared at and saved for when we were little. Music was on and the neighbours were in.

Mother noticed me and gave me a pale smile. I weaved my way to her, feeling that the whole of the stadium crowd had been imported into our living room. Reaching her, I clung to her arm for security. She whispered that George had a two-year contract with Footscray. The periphery! It wasn't what he had hoped for, but it was good. Better and with more opportunities than if he had been stuck in even the best of the Factories' teams.

Mother asked me, 'What will you do now?'

It was strange, her asking me that. I'd thought she hadn't noticed much these last few years—ill all the time, a solemn wrath floating to and from her factory.

'I'm going to try for a bonus.'

She nodded. She must have talked to Aunt Heddie about it.

It was Aunt Heddie who had talked Father into letting me stay on at school these last three years. But Father had never even thought that I could sit for HSC exams and then interview for bonuses, when George wasn't good enough.

The noise ebbed and flowed around us. The party continued, echoing and loud, into the small hours of the morning. Now that George was floating off on a wave of celebration, my personal reef was close.

It was only two days later, when the colour and pleasantness of my brother's success were beginning to fade at the edges, that Father told me he had found me a job. It was a good job, too. Almost full wages because of my good school record and my holiday experience in the factory that had the vacancy. He announced it at dinnertime, pleased and proud at the reflection of his own success. The whole family was there.

All I could do was sit blankly, seeing the cloud of my dreams scatter away, break, and fade.

I couldn't fight against my family publicly. We had tried to always be obedient and it would shatter the whole family and hurt me if I were to say, 'No.'

Aunt Heddie filled the gulf caused by my not speaking.

'I thought she was trying for a scholarship,' she said.

It was the greatest joke of the evening. Even Josh kicked Ann surreptitiously to make sure she caught his grimace. Girls didn't sit for exams. Internal assessments had already assured me a pass. Who needed more than a pass to work in a factory? My twin would sit them alone, in three weeks' time. What did she think I was, a genius?

After the laughter came bitter anger, and the realisation I had enrolled behind everyone's backs. I hadn't wanted to let them down. But where could I have found the courage to tell them?

At that moment, all I wanted was to creep into my room and lose myself in the safety of a book. Only four of us had expected the situation and the air was infused with bewilderment. Mother asked me what I thought. The faces of my family seemed focussed sharply on me.

I looked around slowly, trying to assess the impact of what I was saying. 'Father, surely the factory will hold the job, if it isn't long. And they always say we should improve our education. I can sit the exams then go to work.' My statement was greeted with a relief that I hadn't wished for. If I did get a scholarship, then the battle would begin all over again.

The next three weeks I studied. My whole life was on the line and there was no room to fail. It was humiliating. Once I caught a smirk on a brother's face. Females brought no laurels to the family. Even my sisters avoided my gaze.

I overreacted. For three weeks I resolved to give up painting. My portfolio was ready for the exam, and leisure time could wait. I began studying across the corridor at Aunt Heddie's. It was peaceful there. After about a week of late nights and early mornings, with nothing but black print on white paper, blue characters at the computer terminal, I began to feel the strain. My head felt tight, my brows weighted, and green spots danced over my vision.

One night, Mother crossed the corridor. Quietly she took out the painting Aunt Heddie had packed away only days before. She asked me to finish it for her, so that she'd have something to remember me by when I was gone. It saved me, I think, that painting. It had become harder and harder to have confidence in myself when even the teachers had begun to doubt I would make it. I was up against state-wide competition they told me now, competing against kids born and brought up in pure City areas.

I painted every evening before I went to bed. I was still terrified, scared of the exams, scared of Father, and worst, scared of myself. However, I slept soundly and woke up refreshed. I learned to value the quiet parent. Her confidence helped balance the family's mocking cynicism and Aunt Heddie's worrying and fidgeting. Most of that time is buried deep, an unpleasant memory.

I sat the exams with nervousness and occasional panic, but the interviews I enjoyed. My classmates called them traumatic, and I suppose twelve hours of them ought to be. But for the first time in any exam I found myself faced with people. I didn't give the answers the examiners always wanted, but I enjoyed myself.

I didn't know how well I'd gone. How can a product of the Factories assess the marking system of a group of outsiders? But I came out happy. I felt as if I had found out something about myself, about the people in that room. For all that they were examiners, they were friendly and human, and it was strangely reassuring to know that.

Then it was over, and I went to my production-line job. No one suggested a break, and after hearing my fears and worries, not even Aunt Heddie thought I'd get an award.

It was Mother who brought the letter with my results to the factory at lunchtime. She had taken the day off and, miraculously, had managed to get me the afternoon off. So we went to a park to open it. We just sat for a few minutes. It was that still time between shift changes that lasts maybe fifteen minutes. It was so rare to find a park that wasn't full of people and chaos, that we savoured it.

As the early afternoon workers walked past, I finally opened the letter. I had a scholarship to the University of Melbourne. It covered full board, tuition, fees, and even pocket money. As I handed the slip of paper to Mother, I wondered how the rest of the family would react.

Needless to say, Aunt Heddie was delighted, and so were my teachers. We told them first. Then we went home. No one even asked us whether I'd got anything. It wasn't important. I had a good job and that was my future. Robert had a scholarship too, a small one, to a local Tech, the computer school. He and I had long ago agreed that reform had to come from the top, and the systems that organised the Factories, so he was on his way. Magnanimously Father offered him a larger allowance.

That reminded Robert. 'Did your result come today too?'

There was an uncomfortable silence. No one wanted to tell Robert that it wasn't important.

I grinned, suddenly feeling wicked and adventurous. If I was going to the City, it didn't matter how much of a stir I caused. I told him, yes. And that I had a scholarship.

The silence deepened and changed in quality. Everyone stared blankly at me. I handed the slip of paper to Robert. He looked at, whistled in astonishment, and passed it over to Father. Father read it.

He turned and left the room. Life went on as usual. No one could congratulate me until Father did. The kids were sent to do their homework. Mother went into the kitchen. I went to my room. The silence continued for three weeks. I was edgy.

I suppose I hadn't really considered that Father might refuse to let me go. After all, I was still a minor, and it was his decision. And for all Father's popularity and success he was slow. Oh, it was a deliberate slowness, he was no fool. But he needed time to consider things, to let his brain tick over, to make the right decision. He did not change his mind later either. So I grew cold and scared and began to feel as if the whole world were against me. My education was a deceit and a waste of time. I almost began to feel that I belonged nowhere and was unwanted. At the factory I experienced much isolation and lack of understanding. I looked forward to coming home to the oblivion of late-night reading and sleep. Like any adolescent, I found a way out of my misery in melodrama, creating a glorious martyrdom for myself, the martyrdom of intellect to the stupidity of the working classes.

But at heart I knew that Father honestly felt I would be happier in the Factories than outside, that it would be good for me to play a traditional role.

Underneath it all, I was worried that he did not understand that I wanted to shape my own future.

Slowly the days passed, a monotony of nail-biting and worry. Two days before I had to let the authorities know whether or not I wanted the scholarship, I reminded Father that I had to actually give an answer, that saying nothing was not an option. He asked me then if I really want to go. I said, yes.

For the first time he asked what I would do with a University education. I told him I wanted to teach and to paint. For both I needed proper training, not available in the Factories. He asked to see my paintings and spent the next day pondering them, searching in them for the answers to his questions. It was as if he were deciding on my character, finding out for the first time what his daughter was made of.

The next day he said I could go.

The few days after that were a rush. There was only a fortnight till the semester began. I hurried even more than I had to because I was scared that Father might change his mind. Not that he ever did, but there had been no celebrations. Not even for Robert. This lasted right up to my departure.

Even that was solemn and somewhat tearful. Only my immediate family saw me off. Not like George's huge crowd—he was, after all, a sportsman—with swarms of cousins and aunts and well-wishers. It was dignified, and my heart ached as if I was cutting myself off from the Factories forever.

Several weeks into the semester I received a small parcel from Mother. The letter accompanying it didn't say much, only that she was sending me tokens of something that happened the night of my departure. In the parcel was a mango, crinkled and juicy with ripeness. Tied in a neat bow around it was a cheerfully striped, incredibly gaudy ribbon. And with them was a card of congratulations signed by members of the family, friends and even people from work. Father's scrawl dominated the page.

Reflection

He was reading a novel. It was one of those rare books that carried him outside himself and into another world. Escapist reading was for relaxation of the mind. True escape came from a first-rate work of art. He said this to anyone who asked why he enjoyed Dickens or Dostoyevsky, why he disliked Hardy and seldom looked at bestsellers. Reading to him was a drug; he was addicted. Like writing. Had to write, he told everyone, couldn't stop. And with sweet pride, 'I've even had a story published.'

His days were mostly like anyone else's. Put yourself in his place.

Run through time from your arrival at work until the last bit of paperwork is finished (or left till tomorrow) and you can undramatically catch a train home. Or, if it's Friday, then go home via the pub. Have an extended lunch if you're in the right job, or a few drinks with friends. And the weekends. Some of your weekends must have been like some of his. Saturday—market day. Saturday arvo—football or tea with a friend. Or, when the market was too tempting, an afternoon of slowly nibbling rich cakes and exotic fruits. Maybe a cooking spree in the evening. Maybe not.

John went to Chinatown for his groceries for a bit and tried to teach himself Chinese cooking from books. He'd ask advice at shops and seldom got useful answers. The shopkeeper never knew what he was talking about. Once one explained, apologetically, that she only knew Chinese cooking. But it made a great showpiece for his visiting friends. Especially womankind, slightly surprised that he could cook at all. 'Not your usual bachelor fare, I'd guess,' he'd say to them, the corner of his mind noting their reactions and grinning lightly. Naturally his face didn't grin, it looked suitably self-deprecating.

The reason his life was a bit like yours was because he didn't lack friends, or a social life. His reactions were always acceptable, frequently amusing. So Saturday night was never spent at home, and Sunday morning was mostly spent in bed. Sunday afternoon he'd maybe go for a drive in the country with friends, or to the beach. Occasionally he'd play golf, visit—there was considerable variety.

But not during weeknights or early morning. His time was not his own then. It was ruled by his addictions. Since it was evening now, he was reading. Actually, normally this early in the evening he was scrounging for books. He haunted bookshops of all kinds, watching for the rare gems that could appear. As long as the book didn't actually fall to pieces as he touched it, condition was unimportant. But last Saturday, he had borrowed a book from a friend and, unusually for him, had taken more than an evening to read it. This morning he'd not written a word, much less the four hundred words he wrote every weekday without fail. And he'd almost been late for work.

You see, it was a particularly absorbing book. John always told people that he read to take him out of himself and to see the world properly. This wasn't true at all. He was addicted to books because they took him into himself and he could forget the world. His writing could, I suppose, be called the expression of what he discovered there. That's assuming, though, that there wasn't much to discover. Anyway, the effect this book had on him was electric. It was his mind reflected there, inside it, and he was slowly drowning in it. At first he hated it. After twenty minutes he had put it down and said, 'There has to be a first time for not reading even a hundred pages.' Eight hundred pages of disconnected phrases seemed just too much for him.

But at his desk, the next day, he felt that all he was doing was filling in forms, shuffling papers, answering the phone. Conversation at tea break and lunch was entirely comprised of disconnected ebb and flow. Yes, "disconnected" was the word he used to describe it to himself when he found it unsatisfying. I suppose the feeling happens to all of us.

Anyway, after roaming the library that evening, he came out without a book to read. It sometimes happened that he could not find one to suit his mood. But he had to read; it nagged him and made the back of his mind restless and fidgety. TV didn't help. He had to read.

So he picked up the book again. This time he picked it up in frustration. 'Okay,' he said to himself, 'if I'm going to have to read then I'll just make myself finish this book. It's a test of my mental discipline.' John didn't like feeling that he lacked concentration, you see; it made him feel ephemeral. All of us find reasons to describe the way we skirt around our lives; lack of concentration was John's, just as pocket-sized philosophy is mine.

This led to today. Or now. Well, you know what I mean. The time you started reading this. The time John discovered himself in a book and couldn't draw himself away. It wasn't his personality he discovered (if he had, he probably wouldn't have recognised it) but the pattern of his life. Petty and meaningless, disconnected and lacking depth—he was drawn towards it. I was going to say "like a moth to a flame" but that lessens it somehow, makes it melodramatic. This isn't a story, you know, it's real.

So at three in the morning, he was still reading. Actually, it wasn't so unusual for him to be reading at 3a.m. Book addicts are like that. But it was rare for him not to be turning to the clock every half hour and saying, 'Now I really must be going to sleep.' He didn't even notice the ticking of the clock, much less the time on its face, so absorbed was he.

Finally, the book ran out and slipped down to a snug position next to his pillow. He didn't even notice that the cover bent back, putting a white line down the middle of an orange-tinged picture. Sleep had risen up to meet him, just as the solid people of the book had let him out of their net. The story hadn't let him go, however. It filtered into his dreams, weaving a web around them and through them. Even today John could not tell you how the book finished because of the shape of his dreams that night. And upon arising, he wrote solidly for four hours, only breaking for five minutes to ring work and plead illness. He ate a huge breakfast then crawled into bed and slept again. Then he wrote until words jumbled in his brain and his hand shook from exhaustion.

Sliding into the bedclothes, he pulled the pillows down from the propped-up position and lay there for a half-hour, his mind a white sheet of paper. After a while he realised that this was not precisely a constructive thing to do. Then he realised that he was hungry and hadn't seen anyone for days. Work hadn't counted since the book had trapped him. It had been an enforced rest period during which reading was impossible. Since he didn't feel quite up to talking (or using words at all) he went out for dinner. In fact, he dressed up smartly and went to a place where he could sit down and be waited upon. No, it was not a Chinese restaurant.

It took him nearly an hour to get ready, and another fifteen minutes while he had a cup of coffee and a biscuit to tide him over. John was in one of those vague, imprecise moods where he got everything done. That is to say, he'd put on a tie, make it sit perfectly, then think (his mental voice a monotone), *Isn't it clever, I've put on a tie.*

So he even remembered to take his wallet to the restaurant, without having to remind himself to pick it up. Of course, he had to spend five minutes outside the restaurant looking for it, to make sure he hadn't left it at home.

By the time his meal arrived his eyes were falling from their sockets and his jaw sagged slightly. His skin felt like blotting paper and he ached. From the toe he had stubbed without noticing, to the stomach he had forgotten to feed, to the muffled headache that came from too much sleep: everything about him was a ravening, gnawing pain. It brought him down to earth a bit. Food did the rest.

At first he ate quickly, ignoring the taste, just dampening the throbbing body. Then he ate more slowly, filling the gaping hollow inside him. And at last he ate to taste the fine delicacy of the food, and had another coffee (this time with a liqueur) to finish off. What started as a way of getting mental security and thumbing his nose at his own pedestrian existence, ended as the summit of hedonist luxury. He would've had a second liqueur, but knew he'd feel too guilty about his bank account if he did. John was satiated.

So he went to a movie. It was hollow. He reflected that the liqueur would have been cheaper and more satisfying.

Returning home, he stumbled across what he had written. How could he have forgotten it? Running like a gravel path beneath the surface of his mind was the book. Still and again. When he went to the movie, he had compared it with the book. When he was drowning out the pangs of his body, he was stifling the pangs of the book. So when he reached home, the papers scattered round his bed left him pleasantly surprised.

He began reading. Addicts are like that. No matter how sensible it would be to leave something alone, they can't do it. Words on a page were there, in front of him. He read them. The logic was inexorable. Besides, he genuinely wanted to know what he had written.

Laugh if you will, but in the physical exhaustion of having written and under the psychological domination of that book, he had genuinely forgotten. Slowly, he read.

Eventually, he put it down. Not having reached the end, he didn't know if he wanted to. He hadn't written fiction for once. It was a long screed about self-discovery through fiction.

It was a safe thing to do, John had decided. Like walking through a picture-gallery. You get to choose what you accept, what ideas you want to take; there is no threat, no danger. John, the book addict, had no need to throw himself off a cliff to battle the concept of the instant of death if he could get an author to do it for him.

It was a good essay as far as it went. But for all John's writing practice it was a theorist's essay. A long tale of what writing should ideally do. Challenge without threat, self-discovery without self-destruction. That was the key message.

But John had made the mistake of putting his writing down before he reached the end. If he had done that with the book, halfway into it, then he would have reached this point earlier. It was a cold shock, a splash of ice water on the face. For the first time he saw his addiction clearly and saw its threat. John was immersing himself so thoroughly in books that he had not even realised he was underwater. Reading was no problem. Writing was probably cathartic. But thinking that any individual could not, somehow, pose a threat to him was a mistake. If it was writing that took him inside himself so thoroughly that coming into the rest of the world was like emerging from the sea, then it did not lack danger. If any book, even the greatest work, could make him lose touch with reality, then he could drown.

John realised what he had spent the day doing. He'd been teaching himself to swim.

Mountains of the Mind

In the light of autumn sunset, the maples sing. They chant to the sky a song of red-russet glory. I walk among them and play with words in my mind. Ideas form and leap, little ripples of light in a sparkling sea. Words are not the centre of my life, but I could not imagine walking the autumn sunset without them. I expect they run together deep in my mind. Images floating. Seamlessly joined together like foam on those waves.

Oh dear, that was a mixed-up thought. On nights like this, with the dust-blown autumn wind, and the cold leeching the last of the summer heat, seeping and creeping up through the ground, tinting the trees orange-brown and scarlet, my mind is full of floating images. I wonder what he'll think about it? Other days may be prosaic, organised (though always voluble), but today when my brain imprint (what a rich, pretentious phrase, 'my brain imprint') was taken for the experiment, today is a mirror-reflection day, a time when all my thoughts echo the world through words and phrases. I wonder what he'll think?

Dean entered the psychology laboratory. Why were labs always white and bleak? Mr Helman met him and chatted noisily. Too loud. Trying to reassure him that it was all fine and good. Dean didn't want vague reassurances at all.

'You said you had a demonstration model?'

'Well, it's hardly that. It's a sort of simulation of what happens. Graphic, quite pretty, really, and totally inaccurate. For the newspapers, you see. What you receive is an injection, not large. And you'll be under sedation for it tomorrow, you know that don't you? Good. Well, anyway, you seem to know all about it. Do you really want to see the simulation? A research student thought it up—bright young thing, nearly finished an M.A. under Robbo here. Pretty good idea really. I'll explain while you're watching. See, instead of showing the injection (which we can't do because it hasn't happened yet, ha, ha) or how we take the imprint which no one really believes in anyway, we have two pictures... Wait a second, this is a bit slow running.

'There they are. The blue one represents you, and the yellow one the other person. By the way, I can tell you one thing about him. He's a she. It certainly can't hurt for you to know that in advance. A most definite, organised lady, you'll be pleased to know. She came out as close to compatible as anyone.'

Dean watched as two skull shapes moved towards each other in sharp relief. The background looked very dark as the skulls merged to green. 'You can see why I say this has nothing to do with the actual process. It's a metaphor, I suppose, that's all.

Anyway, you'll have her imprinted into your mind, or chemicals from her mind, rather (don't tell anyone I told you, but the lady herself lives on the other side of the world) for just three hours. If it is successful, we'll work on refining the process, making the imprint for longer, getting subjects to keep logs. Lots of things we ought to do now. But one step at a time, one step at a time. Just as long as we can get grants. Want a cup of coffee?'

The next day Dean settled himself into starched sheets. The last time he'd been in hospital was for his tonsils. Couldn't eat for days. The ice-cream bit afterwards had been a real let-down. Everyone had said how good it would be to eat unlimited amounts of the stuff, but how could you when everything *hurt*. Well, not much pain from this. Hopefully. He shut his eyes and tried to visualise what would happen. First there would be a second's pain from the needle. Then sleep. When he woke up, there would be someone in his mind with him, a passive imprint of a personality. Impossible to imagine. A woman, maybe a girl. What was she like? This thing would be easier for her than for him, he supposed. All she had to do was give the imprint. He had to receive it.

The stiff whiteness of the material against him felt institutional and intimidating. Dean hated institutions of all kinds. But he operated within the system. Had to. There was a logic in behaving as one should. The rewards of good behaviour—he grimaced from the thought he had attached to the entering anaesthetist. In a moment the pinprick of the needle had vanished. Then he was left alone in the room.

Time expanded as he stared at the whiteness around him and drifted slowly, slowly further into the heavy white sheets. It seemed useless to resist their authority.

And then their texture had changed. He was awake. In a tiny room with a bed. Why was he alone? Something was wrong? Through the haze of drug-sleep he tried to think why anything could be wrong.

The yellow brain wasn't there, that was it. Why? They'd told him, he just couldn't remember. Too tired. Easier to contemplate the fibrous texture of the sheets. Tired. That was it.

Helman's voice (deep, a bit confused, rather an exhausting character, so committed...)— 'The imprint will be there, of course, well before you wake up. I suspect you won't feel it till you're a bit recovered from the anaesthetic though. Don't let it worry you.'

Oh. Not important then. Good. Go back to sleep.

The next time he woke up, he woke up completely. And saw, above the end of the bed, perched high, inset in the wall at a strange leaning angle, a TV set. And on the blank screen was a reflection.

...lions roaring within the shadow of lions roaring within the shadow of lions... a reflection is that sort of reality... it isn't reality at all—just an image of it... I see a face, blank-cold, scared, white-tired still... I see it looking at me though my eyes, but it is not me I see... Alan of Lille did not say that the lions reflected real lions, that the shadows reflected real shadows, that they were shadows of truth, only of nature... I am truth, the ice-cold face is a reflection...

'No!' Dean shouted aloud. 'Get out. You're not supposed to think. An abstract idea, that's all. You're a bit of a person, a fragment of personality. Get out of my mind!' But he was rational, and the eeriness wouldn't go. *This is not me I am looking at on the TV screen, it is a reflection of someone else. Something in my mind says so.* His muscles started clenching and knotting as the tension rose within him. No!

He turned his head aside. And there was a picture on the bedside table. *Good. It will distract me.* Hospitals don't have pictures. Dean's eyes focussed on the illogicality of it gratefully. A cat was sitting on a verandah post-stump of an old house. Prosaic. Down to earth. Real, not reflected. *No shadow of lions to haunt me*, he thought.

...warm and alive... it makes the whole picture shadowy and desolate... that cat... emptiness in the wind-whistled rooms... cold greys and browns, lonesome compared with the deep black richness of fur... even in a picture a cat is self-contained... nothing can exist outside the self... a universe of its own, in its mind... there is a part of ourselves that no one can share, the cat says that to us... and behind him the wind whistles in the empty rooms...

The bed smothered him as the alien mind did. Foreignness, strangeness, culture shock. Empty words for a shattering reality. *If I move, do something, maybe the voice won't echo so.*

He had to work hard to get out of bed. Distraction was necessary because of the echo in his brain. And the drug had left a strange weakness in the body. A strong person without either the mind or body he took for granted. In a warm room, Dean shivered. He placed his feet firmly on the cold tile floor. With a desperate certainty, security in the walking, he marched slowly to the door and cautiously turned the knob. It was unlocked!

...the smooth roundness calls to the hand... if it had not turned, it would have denied its nature...

Teeth clenched against this philosophising imprint, he went out into the corridor. It was a private home. Why? He suppressed the question in case the other mind knew the answer. He tried to throw from his consciousness any thought which the other mind might latch onto. There was no logic behind the selection of ideas and phrases in his mind. The oppressive presence of so many words, so much incomprehensible depth, left him bewildered and confused.

As he walked barefoot through a doorway and into a kitchen, he refused to let the images he saw make patterns. A doorway. A sink. Something cold. Not even the word for "refrigerator", much less the pattern for kitchen. Nor would he identify whose kitchen it was. No connecting words or images for the other mind to latch onto.

But it was difficult. It took only a few seconds to realise that. All his life he had been taught to group items, identify them. Hard to break, habit. Too tired and sore. Easier to relax. Forget about making an effort to remain himself.

So he relaxed. Why be worried about confusion? He let the echo grow in his mind until it took on a solidity. And he went to get a glass of water. The anaesthetic had left his mouth feeling like a gibber plain. Beneath his hand, the metal was harsh. Smoothly artificial, it spoke to him of entrapment. The same metal that makes a faucet, creates a cage. He turned it round with a push and swing of the wrist. Water flowed from the tap. He looked at it, she interpreted. Clear and life-giving. It escaped down the plughole in a simple flow. Even when she disrupted the pattern, all escaped. She smiled.

Beneath the smile glimmered Dean's fear. Tears trickled from her eyes. Saltwater. Her mind was at work. Two avenues opened up of themselves as she saw the tears trickle down her face past the smile. And the shadow-personality, that vague feeling of fear, disappeared into the recesses of her mind.

Now a glint of sunlight appeared in her eyes. First, she took off her nightclothes and put on some jeans and a shirt. Then she went out into the bare, bare streets. Her face was alight with joyfulness. The water flowing through the sink went slowly and unceasingly to the sea. She ran like a bird. Underneath her toes, the asphalt burnt in the summer sun like lava. The flight carried her above the heat, but when she stopped to cross the road, the pain reached her. A laugh bubbled out, reluctantly, slightly sardonic. Cathartic burning. Cauterising a wound. Dispelling faint fear. Swallow-like, she fluttered and swooped down the street, her arms wide and beckoning, her lips open in unuttered song. A child, running. Fluting, no words came through. A melody of escape. She reached the end of town and trudged over fields. Time was suspended until that moment.

And there was water again. Tumbling over pebbles, twisting around the rocks, the stream had a permanence and eternity that defied the closeness of the town. In a dry-red country it splashed brown over rocks, flowed crystal over sand. Always there were trees, embroidering the ripples with shade. Looking upwards, the leaves quilt-patterned the sky with green and black and gold. There was movement. Always, always like a child, it was complex and full of life. There was rest. Stillness and simplicity lay behind the sparkle. A Japanese garden with few strokes of line and only a splash of colour. Swirling motion guided its life until it disappeared amongst dank-hanging rocks. The faint shadow in the back of her mind stopped seeking to understand through laboured words. She lapsed into experience—symbolic reality needed no explanations.

Bare feet clung to the rocks precariously as she tried to flow with the stream. Awkward her steps were, staggered and tripping over uneven terrain. Dragged by the current and the restrain of his presence. Toes curled and balanced and the stream flowed on. Jumping and leaping, edging and creeping, it felt forever in the life of the stream before rocks split and shattered and slowly gave way to sand. Not forever. Infinity was the movement of the stream, not of her life. But the hour was long to the clinging feet of the girl-child, with the stream rippling alongside. Stabbed and sharp rocks broke her walk to a whisper. She waded amongst them as the nearby white water did. Both were broken into, defiled and torn apart by the jagged cuts that ripped their movement. Slowly, slowly, the sharpness became smooth and a hobble of misty froth and tired feet dissolved into a flow, deep and untroubled. Branches would fall into the water and splash the calm. Lithe movement of the young body would give way to a hop and a leap. The pace was smooth though, and generally untroubled. The sand continued before the gaze, wide and unbroken, calmly yellow, blind and unseeing. Eyes rose to the horizon where it met the sky amidst a haze of trees.

Sand met her gaze, and behind it, a boy. They smiled at each other and he invited her to play. Sitting down, she began to build with him, piling and piling, randomly and without shape. When there was an absurdly large heap, they looked at each other helplessly and laughed. Then they started shaping it in earnest, making it into a thing worth looking at. She scrambled to her feet and stood way back to look at it. A sigh. There was much work to be done still. Maliciously, in return for the sigh, the boy ran forward and jumped up and down. He spoilt their handiwork with a rush and a sweep of his feet. Then he took handfuls of sand and threw them at first in fun, away from her, then at her feet, then high over her head.

Boldly the sand sprinkled the air. It stung her uplifted face in anger. She ran to the stream and washed herself off, cleansing the bitter smart, smoothing away the pain in a flood large enough to make tears negligible. As the single drop of salt was overwhelmed by the sweet, the bitter remembrance rushed away. She stood high and straight in the shallows, mocking and laughing. In an echo of the stinging sand she flung at him a glint of satiric light, a gleam of droplets.

Baptismal water showered their faces. It laughed in the air, full of the inner glow of clear young sunshine. The still pool of the river-edge was spattered, disturbed as her hand scooped and flung. Yet her laugh retained the hurt of the sand. They could not meet long. The friendship was too close.

As the droplets reached the air, they became spheres of purity. Her eyes caught up by the light, she forgot the shore and the current, and became aware of the clarity of the air and the swift fall of the jewel-dance. Jewels above and below as the glow caught the curves of stones on the river bottom. No sand here. Only gently lit rounded beauty, waltzing with the current.

The water leaped and sparkled, lapped and played around the bare feet. White and floating, despite the joyousness of their movement they were timorous. The stones looked glowing, but underfoot they were hard and glinting. A trial for the soft feet she was used to, but not as difficult for those she had borrowed. So her footsteps became firmer and she waded through the resisting water and down the stream.

Under the surface, Dean half-felt she would guide his thought forever, that this strange flow of words and hinted symbols which had overtaken him, would govern him. Not even the draining, deadly summer heat could sap her vitality.

But at the stream's end, where it flowed into a chasm with a roar and a final twinkle of goodbye, in the noise and uproar of it all, she fell suddenly asleep. And he laughed at the hush in his mind. And he knew where he was.

Home. The room he had found so strange was his own, and the stream began in his own back yard.

And she had faded. Three hours… It was a short time after all. They had said so. What they had not said was more important.

On the pretty computer picture the brains had been the same size. But inside his mind Dean had felt restricted, as if there was a gap between his reality and her reality within it, a gap which couldn't possibly exist. And she had changed. Become like him a bit more. The first moments were so bewildering… but after that, well, he had almost enjoyed it! Except for the words. A game, that was it, maybe she played games with words. Yet how could she develop and change? An imprint surely could not. But they had smiled at each other, built a sandcastle. And quarrelled, wordlessly. She used so many words, yet needed none to smile, or start a fight.

There were still areas of her mind which were like the wind-whistled house behind the cat—inaccessible. A photograph where what counted was substance, empty echoes in a dark room. Lions roaring within the shadow of lions. How many pockets of shadow could another mind contain? And would the echo leave him, ever, even though the imprint had faded?

Dean shivered again. This time it was from the cold of the water he had been sprinkled with. Around him was security.

Part Two

DNA Magic (Little Boxes 2)

I wish it were made of ticky-tacky, Isla thought yet again, as she plunked her box on the desk. She had documented nine boxes and thousands of incidents and was no closer to finding any rational pattern in them. The family story was that inheriting the boxes was one thing and magic was another: gender mattered a bit and genes mattered a lot. She'd found most of the boxes in museums. They'd been stolen for their magic, or lines had died out and they became nothing but boxes. Ancient black boxes. She wished those ancient black boxes acted like modern ones from airplanes and had recordings of their past. Or maybe she wished that this was her particular skill. It wasn't.

Isla had stopped looking at the museum boxes. At first it had been exciting, opening the boxes and accessing the magic and having strange things happen. But then she'd opened the one that was infamous for the incident at the Royal Albert Hall. Simply opening it and humming a bit of a tune in (what she thought) memory of the incident had caused everyone within earshot (except herself) to be raced to hospital. Barely dead, then barely alive. One family, she had decided at that point. All the owners of boxes had to be related in some way. She didn't need to test other boxes. Her own was enough. And maybe DNA tests.

Everyone else had theories. Three boxes were still in private hands. Three known boxes. The unknown boxes were hopefully totally dead and simply valuable ornaments, but whenever one appeared, she checked it out and added the data to her collection.

Originally, she was going to produce a reveal-all documentary. Now she wondered if a novel would be more believable.

'Not everyone who inherits a box inherits magic,' suggested one of the owners, helpfully. He had developed what he called 'a minor magic, not worth documenting' and had translated it into a successful television career. Only he didn't claim to have translated it. He claimed to be a genius at culinary performance. His dishes always came out, and always looked good and never wilted under the lights of the stage, screen or photographer.

Isla's own talent involved bringing the dead to life and it bloody annoyed her. Except when she'd killed everyone in earshot with the Albert Hall box, of course. That was the only time she was happy that she had this talent. Otherwise she'd be a murderer. Much better to revive the barely dead than to murder people.

Much better still if she'd never started her research in the first place. If Uncle Tobias hadn't given her the damn box—'Because you're less likely to do damage with it than your idiot sisters,' he had said, on his deathbed. When she discovered her talent, she'd been tempted to bring him back to life and make him answer the horrible legacy.

She *had* been tempted. Life (or afterlife) made her realise that bringing her uncle back from unsavoury non-existence to his crime-polluted life (one never asked Uncle Tobias what he'd done with his day, for one never wanted to know about it) was a bad, bad idea. Not as bad an idea as calling him names, as her younger sister had done, but close.

Zombies were her least favourite thing and yet she had the special gift to surround herself with them whenever she chose. She avoided cemeteries. When the dead (especially Uncle) didn't rise and look at her with a hungry adoration, she felt she could survive.

'Was Pandora one of us?' That was her first note. The boxes definitely dated to the preclassical world. All the museums said so. She littered her huge pile of notes with small despair. It was all too much.

But it wouldn't be. She was resolved. Soon she'd know enough to handle the box. Her last note would be written any moment. Or maybe in an hour.

In an hour, Freda was coming over with her own box, and they were going to share their most recent notes. Get to the bottom of it. Turn this mess into a miracle of understanding. Research magic into oblivion.

It was only three days ago that she'd discovered that her girlfriend was also a cousin. Genealogy had delayed the studies and they'd discovered that the relationship was so many generations ago they couldn't actually find it, but they believed in it. Freda believed in it. Isla asked, 'But what if there were half a dozen families given different boxes? What if I can only get results out of certain boxes?'

'You get results from every damned box,' her true love pointed out, kindly. 'Unlike me. It's not my box that's our last check, it's my bloodline. And that might lead to results. If we don't get those results, we'll get drunk,' Freda had promised. 'Something I've found out means that… well… I can't say yet. I want to be very, very certain. It's stupid. Just stupid. If I'm right, though, we can appeal. Your knowledge…'

Isla couldn't see how her knowledge could help anyone appeal to anyone about anything. She was the ancient history side of things and Freda was the genetics. Science and history in perfect balance.

'I'll see,' she'd promised.

'I'll see' and 'We'll see' was all she could say to anything that involved tomorrow or the day after. Normally she'd offer Freda more than a cagey agreement. Freda gave her balance in other ways than through the intellect. There was a ring in a drawer that had been waiting for the government to approve marriage. Now marriage was possible, Isla was petrified. 'We'll see,' was the best she could do.

Isla took out her notebook and added the nightmare stories of coming out. Some of the family was fine with her sexuality and some less so. Some of her friends had been adorable and some had never spoken to her since. She hadn't come out to most of them about the zombies yet. Only to Freda.

The zombies were different. She didn't want to think about them, but, honestly, she had to. The way they'd shifted from looking to grabbing. The way she'd become a sex object.

She shuddered and put down the pen. How could she even consider marriage?

It was easier for people who had all the variants of love and desire reflected in movies and books. They'd seen it all on the silver screen. Their fears. Their hopes. Their dreams. Never their zombies. Not once.

The groping wasn't the worst of it. These zombies weren't bloody messes. They didn't have eaten skin and flabby mouths. They were simply not all there.

Maybe they were spirits and not zombies? This she wrote down.

Maybe their bodies were turning corporeal due to her ability. Souls that stayed with the body after death and slowly wafted into nothingness, given physical form might be rapacious. Interested in her. Greedy to share life. Passionate about sharing her life. If she wanted a harem she could have a spirit harem. But she didn't. Freda was more than enough.

'If I write really good notes, Freda can read the bloody things. I don't want to explain this. Zombie romance. Or maybe zombie sex addiction.'

She felt guilty. In a perfect world, she wouldn't use the word "zombie"—for they weren't zombies. She would use the correct word for the correct type of soul. But they squicked her out. She didn't feel any of the lust for them that they obviously felt for her. Her simple response was the kind of political incorrectness she generally abhorred.

Isla wondered if anyone else had been squicked out in that precise way? Certainly some of the other boxed-in had been repulsed or had sublimated their talents. The desiccated orchestras and audiences (same box, three generations of ability) had turned her off classical music entirely and she'd avoided even going near the Albert Hall after she'd read the transcripts of all the banned news stories. Then she went into the damned place to test it out. Understanding, she thought, was a perilous tool.

A few minutes later, she was trying to explain.

Freda had walked in the door saying, 'Talk! I need to know what you've found.'

'But…'

'I have charts. And data. Much good stuff. Tell me all your latest and I'll see if I have answers.'

And so Isla squicked herself out twice in an hour, trying to explain.

'All the zombies are female?' Freda asked.

'They're not zombies. Just... I don't have a word for them yet. I've matched them with those Jewish souls that stay with dead bodies. Did you know that Jews have three souls?'

'We'll use zombies.' Freda was dismissive of cultural issues that didn't feed into her science. One had to love her anyhow. 'And it could just be your fascination with all things ancient that makes you want to explain things using this Jewish soul thing. It's folklore. We're living in the real world.'

'Anyhow, they're not all female,' Isla responded, feebly. She was not in the mood to argue with Freda about folklore and mythology and their obvious link with the boxes. This would come. Just not yet. She made a point she *could* make without getting into an argument about religion. 'Just to be accurate, I'm not lesbian. You are. I'm not.'

'What?'

'Don't look so worried. I fall in love with people. Not gender. You're my true love. It's simple. I don't know if I'm bi or if I am my own sweet solution to human suffering. I'm monogamous. That's what counts.'

'But the gender of the person you're monogamous about isn't at all important to you.' Freda spoke slowly, working out something important.

'Yes it is, in its way. I don't make love to you as if you're a bloke. I make love to you. Yourself. No one else,' said Isla, impatiently. 'And this isn't related to anything box-like. Just us.'

'Actually, it may be. Something in my research… Look, I've got to sit on this for a bit. First I need to sort out what it means to me, personally. And then there's the study. Does it change anything? That's the big thing.'

'And it may?'

'In the study, most certainly. With me? Honestly, I'm not sure. I've… I…' She floundered, then became defensive. 'I didn't even think you were like that. I thought you were like me.'

'It's like coming out again,' Isla said, measuredly. 'With you having to think about me as if you didn't know me. Which you did. I mean, which you do. I haven't changed.'

'No, you haven't,' said Freda, slowly. 'And I didn't mean to put you through that again. Oh God, my experience was bad enough. I swore I'd never… but…'

Isla thought of the ring in the drawer as if it belonged to a distant world and time. 'It's okay,' she said. 'Do what you need to. I'm still here.'

Isla was so busy being good and tactful that she didn't ask about the tests. Freda was so busy trying not to react badly to Isla not being quite what she'd thought, that she simply left the reports on the table. Over the next fortnight the papers were moved from table to chair to dresser to sideboard and back to the table until Isla finally admitted that Freda wasn't going to turn up the way she had for the last year.

When Isla looked at the papers, the first thing she discovered was that she couldn't tell if Freda was related to her at all. DNA was outside her knowledge zone. The second was that there was a note on her report, asking her urgently to ring a number. It was too late for urgent, but Isla rang anyway. Normally she wouldn't. Normally she'd find out a lot more about the owner of the number before ringing. Week

One had been the week of the Great Fear. This week was the week of the Great Uncaring.

She didn't permit the Great Uncaring to enter her voice as she explained the note.

'Oh,' said a bright voice on the phone. 'The boss wanted to see you. Personally.'

'I don't really want to see anyone right now,' said Isla. 'I didn't give any permission to look for diseases and there's nothing in there to talk about.'

'He says he knows you.'

I've lived in Brisbane too long, thought Isla. She was going to leave. But then Freda had turned up. At first it was Freda and her box, and then it became Freda above all else. And it should've been Freda on the phone. Isla cantankerously agreed to a meeting at the State Library café. That had been her meeting place since she got involved with the boxes: it was open and safe, and the Library had been her refuge ever since she was a child.

Laila was the name the boss-woman gave her, but not her real name. She was glamorous and self-possessed and expected everyone to love her, instantly. 'My real name is irrelevant,' she said, dismissing that part of herself with a wave of her hand. 'I call myself after the Hebrew night, dark and splendid and riveting.'

'How can I help you?' This was Isla's polite voice. She'd learned it during her polite days, before she grew into herself. Laila looked too much like Isla herself, but it was her name that told the truth. Whatever Laila wanted, someone was going to suffer. Isla daringly asked a follow-up question before Laila could lead her astray. 'Do you expect everyone to fall in love with you, by the way? Just out of curiosity. Because I won't, you know.'

Laila looked as if the world's core had been stolen from her private acre. She looked as if Isla had accused her of larceny. She looked… ordinary.

Isla smiled to herself and excused her joke. 'It wasn't funny, I know. It was just that you're dressed so splendidly…' Isla knew the answer to her question and would stay clear of this woman, no matter what she offered: she could afford the sop to the woman's ego that would allow her this.

'I'm sorry, I missed the joke.'

There was a pause, then Isla prompted. 'Can I help you?'

'Yes,' said Laila. 'Yes, I believe you can. I've been following your research. I want you to give me that black box of yours. It's mine.'

'Sorry?' Isla wondered if she should be worried about being stalked, or about something else. Since she had two boxes she'd been given and one she'd inherited, she didn't even know which box Laila meant. Maybe the stalking wasn't that close?

'You bought it from a stall in Petticoat Lane, five years ago. It was stolen from my mother.'

'I remember.' Isla's eyes went hard. She'd been chatting about her research with this bloke and he'd pulled out a box and practically begged her to have it. 'They're going to be upset with me for getting rid of it, but they'll hurt other people if they have it,' he'd said.

She let her eyes pretend friendship. This was the least troublesome of the boxes, but not all family members deserved the inheritance, after all. Laila and her mother had a different sort of transformational skill to Isla's own. They transformed prize possessions into dross, then took those possessions for nothing, reconfigured them and sold them on the antiques market for a fortune. Many generations of bad dealing had been supported by that box. Isla had tested the box: she could see no pattern in how things changed, other than they went from gold to dross to gold again. She didn't care. This particular box was better in a museum, and it would be, very soon. Time to lie with style.

'It was the most extraordinary thing,' she said, 'but I donated it to the National Museum of

Australia. Let me give you their details. All you have to do is prove it's yours and they'll return it to you.'

This was the best she could think of on the run. It was there now, at least, being inspected. She knew they'd take it, given its history. Isla was thorough in her research. So was Freda. Not hearing from Freda worried her.

'Thank you,' said Laila, caught in a bind. 'I was going to ask your girlfriend about it. I understand she has a box, herself.'

'I'm sorry, I don't think she can help you. Go to the museum. And, to be honest, I'm not sure about her box. There are a lot of imitations around.'

Freda's box belonged to Freda's family without any doubt, and yet Freda hadn't done anything with it. Maybe by choice, maybe by blood. Mostly by choice. Freda was fascinated by the boxes and even more fascinated with the idea of going to her grave never having used one. This she said whenever she was drunk. It was her special boast. *God, Freda is adorable*, thought Isla. She gave the details to the museum and excused herself, claiming work.

Two hours later, she was interrupted by a phone call. It was Freda's neighbour.

'It's very odd,' he explained. He never complained, but he always explained. Today, with less detail than usual. 'She left a note under my door.

Knocked. And ran. The note says to ring you. Someone called Laila is with her and she says everything is wrong.'

'That's very odd,' replied Isla.

'I said so.' He was glum.

'You did. Thanks for the message. I'll come right round.'

'Bring a gun,' he suggested.

'A gun?'

'I don't like the look of the other woman. I saw her on the stairs.'

'Nor do I,' said Isla. 'I've got a better idea. I promise I'll bring something.'

'And keep me out of it. I'm a peaceful man.'

'You're a good neighbour. Thank you.'

He really was a good neighbour. He'd put up with the experimenting they'd done with the boxes. While she thought, Isla packed. Her family's box was the smallest of them all. The other one she had was larger. If she was right, she'd need both of them.

Twenty minutes later she was turning the key in Freda's lock. She walked in and looked around. Nothing in the living room. There was, however, something moving on the balcony. She walked towards it and waited behind the curtain.

She heard Laila's voice say, 'One last time.' She sounded unhappy. 'Give me your box, or I'll throw you off this balcony.'

'Don't do that,' said Isla, appearing at the open door. 'She doesn't have it.'

'What?'

Freda's face looked relieved, then worried.

Isla wanted to wink. 'I'm the one who has the boxes.' She pulled the larger one out of her pocket and it sat on her outstretched hand, looking innocuous and sucking up all the light.

'What does it do? I need to know.'

'I don't know what my box does,' said Freda. 'My grandmother says it kills people, so we've never opened it.'

'It's like that British one, then.' Laila sounded happy. She took the box from Isla. 'Let's go inside.' She shut the sliding door after them and Isla wondered if she herself had just done something particularly stupid. 'You're the one who's been doing the researching?'

Isla nodded.

'And your girlfriend helped? Good. That makes this much simpler. Her body can be my blackmail.'

She stood so that she leaned directly into Freda's face, flipped the lid open and blew across the top. A light grey dust flew into Freda's mouth and eyes and nose, and she coughed. Laila clicked the box closed just as Freda slumped to the floor.

'That's what I thought,' Laila said. 'It doesn't need music.'

'How did that happen? She fainted.' Isla looked again, and her love's face was pale and she was not breathing.

'She's dead. The mummification came from the music, but the death comes with any use. I've been working on this for years. Now I have the box. And it works. See you.' And she strode towards the door.

The moment Laila's back faced Isla, Isla took out her own box, flicked it open, and, bending over Freda, blew across as if the gesture would breathe life into her lungs. She slipped the box back into her pocket—it was only visible for a second.

Freda coughed again. Laila stopped just short of the door and swivelled round. She saw Isla helping Freda sit up.

'My spirit didn't go very far,' she said to Isla. 'I could see everything. I think there's something in that argument of yours about Jewish souls.'

Laila turned to face the voices.

Isla smiled, then straightened. She looked across and up at the tall woman who had murdered the love of her life. 'I rang the police on the way,' she said. 'They told me they'd call my mobile the moment they were downstairs.' Her mobile phone behaved delightfully and buzzed at that exact moment.

As Laila opened the door, Freda tackled her and brought her down. She grabbed the box and handed it back to Isla, then she held tight to Laila herself. 'I hope you were right about the police,' she said.

'I have no idea what we're doing now,' said Isla. 'Today's a bit of a mixed day.'

'You know where my box is,' Freda said. 'Get it.'

She looked so determined. Isla wasn't going to point out that she'd never used it or that they had apparently different DNA so it was quite possible she had never used it or… she brought the box in. Freda was having trouble holding Laila, so she hurried.

'Get my headphones. The noise-cancelling ones. Both sets. One set on me, one set on you. Then use the damn box. And hurry!'

Isla hurried. Hidden under the earphones, she opened the box, saw nothing inside, and closed it again, wondering what this one did.

Laila had stopped struggling. She was perfectly alive, but her face had lost its emotion. Then the emotion came back, and it was different. She was puzzled. Freda let her go. Laila looked at both of them, shook her head, said, 'I need to find my mummy,' and walked straight out the door.

They took off their earphones and looked at each other.

'Coffee first, I think,' said Freda. 'And thank God you're still yourself.'

'How could I not be me?'

Freda pulled her close and held her a very long time. 'I didn't know. The DNA tests and you coming out—I was just a bit... fraught.'

'The DNA tests?'

'Yeah, well. Dad did parlour tricks with the box when I was a kid. When I was ten, there was a children's party. The biggest ever. Everyone who knew everyone in the whole town. It wasn't a big town. And it was the best party. We each have our own memories from after the box was opened. Memories were split and shared and went crazy. Years later Dad told me he was the one with the box when we all woke up, and he used it one more time to check he had the gift, then he put it away. When he told me about it, he said he'd leave me the box when he died. Which he did. As you know. Only... he wasn't my father. Not before that afternoon.'

'Oh,' said Isla. 'And that explains why you had me do it.'

'You're not human.' Freda's words rushed out of her as if a dam had broken. 'Everyone who can use the boxes has something… I can show you where it is on the charts. I can't explain it.'

'So you want me to leave you? Or not? I'm very confused. I love you. But I'm not human and you didn't speak to me for—'

'Hell,' interrupted Freda, 'I love you. But you're not quite human and I'm human.'

'This is like you being queer and me being not-quite queer. It either matters or it doesn't. To me, you're always Freda. The question is, I guess, whether to you, I'm always Isla.'

'Hell, yeah. But we should get married before it becomes illegal for me to marry someone from a different species. This government didn't want us to be married once. I wouldn't put it past them to make it impossible a second time. There's just one thing,' said Freda.

'What is it?'

'Don't tell anyone I'm a bit zombie, yeah? And maybe we should adopt.'

Happy Faces for Happy Families

I have twenty-one grey hairs. Twenty-one. I have counted them over and over again. Not that I mind going grey, but it's such a surprise to me. It reminds me of things that I had forgotten, I suppose. Or things that I'd rather I had forgotten.

Mostly it reminds me of that day when I was nine-going-on-fifteen. I was so certain that I was almost a teenager that I actively prepared for acne by staring at my face in the mirror for interminable lengths of time every day. Encouraging my zits along. Longing for that growth spurt, for my voice to deepen, for strange changes to warp my body into its next phase.

Mum shouted in the background, 'Phil, you have fifteen more minutes and then you start your homework, or else.'

I stared and waited for my free time to evaporate. It's funny how sometimes you remember the exact look of things and the exact feel of things and the exact thoughts going through your mind. One moment when everything clings to memory, from the polish on my skin to the fearsomely clean bathroom reflected from behind me.

Me staring at the mirror, wanting to be like my brother. I wanted to be able to sing in that cracked, sexy way, and to look across a room with a totally impenetrable gaze. I yearned for girls to glance sideways across the street at me the way they did at him, and for the teachers to stop me and have a bit of a yarn about this and that. I didn't want to *be* him—I just wanted his voice and his dark eyes and the girls to admire me.

It was a very clean mirror and it most definitely showed pink Phil, with no trace of Ben.

At that second Dad walked past, talking to Ben. 'I am going to have to rethink my formula—there was no change at all last time. No movement.'

Ben murmured something as the voices moved down the corridor, '…mechanical failure, maybe,' were the only words that I could make out.

I focussed on my face again—nothing to be learned from half a conversation.

The half-conversation was typical, because the Big Secret was Dad and Ben. Never me. Wisps of technobabble and mathematics wafted past, excluding me. Just as the locked door of the machine room excluded me. All I got was one glimpse when that door was left open by mistake: I walked around for days trying to get a second peek. I could not make head or tail of it, but everything was impressively large and complicated.

The other reason the Big Secret affected Ben more than me was because I was with Mum for my early years, and he was with Dad. And then they made up, and we all moved in with Dad. And so Ben knew things that I never could.

And here is another memory. An evening in the life of Phil, age nine. Mum cooked dinner and heard all about school. Lots to tell. Ben was floating around somewhere: he did that. Occasionally he would wasp through the kitchen with a caustic comment.

Dinner was late because Dad was late: that was nothing new. Nor was me being hungry! I got myself a glass of milk and snuck a handful of sultanas from the jar Mum kept on the cupboard. My hand was getting bigger and I had trouble getting it out in time before Mum spotted me.

Eventually Dad came home with a friend. We ate in silence, because children did not talk at the table when work colleagues appeared. Even when there was not quite enough food to fill one child in particular. Dad must not have rung to tell Mum he was bringing someone. Again. No one ever commented on how late he was, or suggested the rest of us could eat earlier. After dinner he and Ben went their ways and I helped with the dishes. I got sprung bad when my hand did get stuck in the sultana jar. Mum gave me a slice of bread and butter, then told me, 'Half an hour till homework. Then bed.'

Of course, I complained.

And now the mind images make sense. I realise that Dad was Teflon Man. Not human enough for anything to stick. Ben was the centre of the universe, and Dad was the lump of soil we all went around to get to Ben.

Today a dam broke—or a damn memory broke—and my mind flooded with blame. Those grey hairs did it.

My mind skipped forward to the bathroom again. That mirror moment was the vortex of my remembering. It's as if Dad and Ben were still talking in code and disappearing to the machine room.

Happy Families helped hide what Dad was doing. All of us fronted up at Dad's work from time to time and played the Happy Families game. It was important to Dad, Mum said, and Ben said it was a cool thing to do, so I rolled along merrily. I was just a little wheel in the Happy Family. Round, pink, contented-looking, *obedient* Phil.

It wasn't a Happy Family. It was supposed to be happy and we did all the good behaviour and show-off things that normal happy families do, but it wasn't. We never talked about why.

Secrets. Always secrets.

Dad's job was a secret. Ben's illness was secret. Ben's illness was a special sort of secret, though—an open secret, something we all knew about and none of us could say aloud.

When Ben had a high pain day, I would play spaceships soundlessly.

I knew when his high pain days were. I could tell. Doesn't matter how many secrets Dad had, I knew all about Ben's pain. I could read it when his movements muted and slowed, and I could read it when his eyes looked strained. By that day when I stared at myself in the mirror, I could gauge Ben's personal misery to the nth degree, and each time his pain went up a notch, I took my exuberance down a notch, out of respect.

The mirror day was a high pain day. I had seen it during dinner when I was supposed to be staring at my plate politely.

I looked in the mirror and hated it. I hated every minute of him hurting. I also hated having to walk to school by myself. I hated the fact that no one looked at my school projects properly, or asked me what I wanted for dinner.

Secrets. I hated secrets.

I was so full of hate that when a teacher once told Mum how sweet I was I nearly gagged. In my mind Miss Jones was bombarded with missiles from my mental spaceships. They were in close formation around her head and they shot nuclear-powered darts through her ears and atomic missiles into her eyes and mouth and up her nostrils to land in her brain and cause her great agonies. Her skull haemorrhaged holocaust.

That was how I coped. Science fiction. Anything with a spaceship. And derring-do, there had to be derring-do. I was the best Lensman of all and I saved the whole family from the villains of the universe. I was Luke Skywalker and Captain Kirk combined. I was adventure. I was daring. I controlled my destiny.

I was *Lost in Space.*

I turned my thoughts for a minute to starships and dogfights instead of zits. Being lost in space meant I could ignore Ben's voice continuing downstairs.

'I am sure that the monitor is not working properly,' he said. 'I could feel the shift, even though your records don't show anything.' Then the door slammed and they were shut in the machine room again, playing with their secrets.

Mum was sorting out Ben's medications downstairs. Mum took care of Ben and put on a happy face (Happy Faces for Happy Families—

nothing less was acceptable) and pretended not to fuss.

When she put on her happy face, I looked the other way. And sometimes I was where I was at that moment—in the bathroom with the door locked. Lonely as all hell.

Then the mirror did something unexpected. This is why I remember it, of course. I must have stared at myself wistfully a thousand times with nothing to hold on to, so those memories have seeped away.

I was expecting to see a sprouting hair or two, or maybe the redness of zits *in potentia*. Promises of cool to come. No, there I was, nothing cool about me. Just me. Pink and scrubbed and hopeful. As I eyeballed myself, I had to cross and uncross my eyes to make my vision clearer. I did this because it seemed that something was going wrong with the mirror, or with my eyes—I had to be certain which it was. It really looked as if I was seeing a double image. A face outlined around my own. Bigger, less chubby, but a familiar shape. My face. Older and less pink.

I was mesmerised. My imagination was taking me to a place I had not been before, and I had no idea how I was supposed to react.

Then the shadow-face spoke. It had a voice! Deep and resonant and, yes, maybe a little sexy. I admired that voice.

'Phil, is that you?'

I hate it when my jaw drops. I still hate it now, but back then it was humiliation to die from. Open mouths on round pink faces look like girls' dolls. *Yuck*, I thought to myself. I couldn't say a word.

'Phil, listen to me. I don't have long.'

I felt so stupid. A total idiot. All I could do was stare. Somewhere in my mind I noticed that the background to his face wasn't the white of the bathroom—shades of the machine room had overlaid my reflected pristine tiles. And his face was still mine. I own that face and I would recognise it anywhere. Except… except that it was older, and there were other differences. My face with Ben's eyes. My face with Ben's pain. So, no, I did not move. I could not move. I could not answer. But I could listen.

'Damn, but I hope you are hearing me, Phil,' my face said. 'You look like a stuffed dummy. A stuffed dummy in a shiny white coffin. Dammit. I haven't any time to waste—Dad'll be back any minute.'

He paused.

'Look, Dad is playing silly buggers with space-time and he thinks his children were conceived purely to serve as his personal guinea pigs. He didn't start in on me, on you, whatever, until Ben died. I hope I have worked this out in time. I hope I got the bloody settings right. Listen…' And his face focussed on mine, all agony and sincerity. 'Don't let him take you into the machine room. Not now, not ever. You do *not* want to know the Big Secret. Got that? You do not want to know the Big Secret.'

His enunciation was simple and over-clear, as if he was speaking to an imbecile.

'What did you say about Ben?' I finally croaked.

'He is still alive?' that deep voice sounded faintly surprised.

I nodded.

'Well bully for him.' That other me was callous. 'It's too late to help him anyhow.'

I loathed this new voice of mine. Deep voices should be warm, and this was as cold and lonely as the moon.

'Just keep out of the machine room. Don't go near it. Dammit, that's the door.'

My mouth was rounder than my face when the image fractured, and I was left alone with the bathroom.

There was only one thought in my mind. It was such an ocean of a thought that I let it drown me. My reactions swept me into a zone I had never owned before. I never want to own it again. Big brothers do not die.

In that zone, my mind screamed, and my body copied it. My mind threw things, and my body copied it. My mind cried, and my body sobbed until I was hysterical and had to be injected. I noticed the injection with only a small part of me, but I didn't care. I just didn't care. I had to scream and cry and beat everyone with my fists until the world became sane again.

I wanted that mirror-self to come back and say, 'I lied, ha ha. Got you good, huh?'

I wanted to be home, not in a house of Secrets and Happy Families.

Some morsels of memories remain from the hours before the injection: my supper on the floor, Dad throwing his chair against the wall, Mum crying. I remember slowing down for a little and starting to be myself again. That was when I noticed that Ben wasn't there and I started screaming, 'He is dead, he is dead, he is dead.'

Mum tried to tell me he was just resting upstairs. But I couldn't stop screaming.

And that is all I can tell you. I can't connect it. I don't want to connect it. I don't know why I am even remembering this much.

The next day I woke up to Dad shouting, distantly. I made myself small as a mouse since that was how big I felt after the unexpected havoc of the day before, and I crept out of my room and towards the voices. Trying to recapture the moment now, I do remember me feeling a little rodent-smug. I had not played Happy Families. I had been injected with something! The small sickness in my stomach was like a war wound. I puffed my chest out a bit as Phil-the-Mouse scuttled downstairs.

Mum was in her room, and I hid behind the door where no one could notice me. I could see her folding clothes. She seemed very placid given the fact that Dad was shouting from across the bed. I couldn't see Dad, but I hoped he was red-faced. He certainly sounded red-faced. He sounded like he had looked the night before, when he had thrown that chair.

You know, until then, I had not known that Dad had emotions. And now I knew that Dad could lose it better than anyone I had ever known in my whole life. It was strange to find out that Teflon Man threw tantrums.

Finally, Dad sputtered to a halt. The folding of clothes had obviously got the better of him.

Then Mum started talking. Her voice was inexorable. There was no room to argue.

She explained stuff I had never really understood, like us being Happy Families for Ben. It made sense. Then she said something surprising. Apparently, there had been a condition attached to us moving in with Dad and Ben. I was astonished to hear this.

'We had an agreement,' she said, 'that Phil and I would go straight home the minute I found anything wrong with him. I am keeping you to that agreement. We will be gone by the end of the week.'

Dad tried to argue. The main thrust of his argument was that I was just a spoiled child, a mother's boy who needed the discipline he himself had been given, and that he had given Ben.

Mum kept folding and folding and folding. Then she said, 'I don't give a damn what you think. Phil and I are leaving in three days' time. And I have already told Ben that he can come too, if he wants.'

'He needs his treatments,' was the first articulate thing my father said.

'I will take him to specialists near home. We will get a second opinion, too. I do *not* believe he is getting any better. I have listened to you for far too long. Your degrees aren't worth a *damn* if you can't see how sick your son is.' There were such depths of bitterness in Mum's voice.

Too late. It was all too late. While Mum and Dad were arguing and while I was peeking from behind the door, Ben vanished from our lives, softly and quietly. His movements went from muted and slow, to entirely still.

My screams had failed.

And we took two extra days to leave, because of the funeral.

It was my first funeral. Every second is still etched into my nightmares. The thing that hurt most was realising that it was my brother, Master of Cool, who was being stifled by the red-brown earth. But the clearest image is of Dad upright, at the far side of the grave, never crying, never looking across at us. I can still feel Mum holding my hand so tight she bruised me, and me squeezing her back just as hard.

Sometimes I wonder. I wonder if I had not screamed and screamed and screamed and screamed if Ben would still be alive. Would he have been alone in the machine room at just that moment? Would there have been help for him?

And other times I wonder what would have happened to me if I had not met myself in the mirror. Would I have vanished, too?

For years I waited to see if I would fade like my brother—I waited every day for shadows beneath my eyes and for the constant company of fatigue. Eventually waiting transmuted into normal life. I stopped looking in the mirror for pallor. I stopped looking in the mirror for shadows. I stopped looking in the mirror for future echoes.

And now I am older than I was in that mirror, and nothing has happened to me. Nothing.

That face in the mirror changed everything for me, you know. It only changed things, though, because I thought it was me. I kicked and screamed and fought and fit and got us away from Dad. At that moment in my life, I knew Ben was dying, and I knew I would die too if we stayed in that house with Dr Mad Scientist. Or was I rebelling against Ben hurting? I don't know anymore.

Either way, it was Dad. All Dad. I didn't know it was possible to hate and love and not forgive all at once until I was nine and met myself in a mirror.

Okay, so that is a self-pitying dramatisation. I know it. But that is my mood. I didn't just go to the mirror and discover grey hairs. Life is not so merry.

My damn memory broke when I opened the paper this morning and saw that Dad had died. 'A genius, whose ground-breaking work on theories of space-time and alternate realities have changed the way we view existence. Scientific circles will particularly remember him for his controversial paper on possible adjustments human bodies might make to the non-lineal experience of time.'

Finally, I know what the Big Secret was. I could find out more about it by reading those world-shattering publications, but I think I may give it a miss. Instead I am going to focus on deleting the memory entirely—never thinking again of me with haunted eyes, dying from too much Happy Families.

Twenty-one grey hairs—twenty-one today. I am alive.

Memo

You expect me to classify this? It is a fragment of a book. Tourist rubbish, old and full of puffery. Twenty-first, twenty-second century, I don't know. Something Southern. I won't have a thing to do with it. Give it to someone who gives a damn about working in these bloody archives.

From: Your bored underling who would put in his resignation tomorrow if anyone else would take him

To: Supervisor Trakant (aka Supervisor Total Idiot who actively seeks out fragments of books that ceased to have meaning five hundred years ago)

… enjoy its sublime green plains and tranquil lakes. You will never forget your experience.

The coast is not well-known. It lacks the exquisite beauty and vast horizons of the inner sea. In its place, you will find intriguing hints of the past that was Old Australia.

Sydney is worth the visit. As you hover overhead, its big highways reflect the 'Emerald City' label it proudly bore in the twentieth and early twenty-first century. The highways are now rich green with algae and seaweed, and gleam pale-phosphorous at night.

From the comfort of a glass-bottomed boat you can pay a friendly visit to Ancient Suburbia, with its quarter-acre blocks and its decaying houses. Clever navigation will take you round Sydney skyscrapers, not too close, because of the danger of falling glass. In the sunset the glass and sea dance with the dolphins and remind you that once millions of Australians lived in this Lucky Country.

Fearful

'You're full of fear. Fearful.'

'Oh, just shut up,' she said.

This was the seventh time he'd done one of his clever plays on words. Except that they weren't clever, and they weren't words she wanted to hear—timid, scared, afraid, chicken, fainthearted, spineless. His insults were always in sevens. He played on them. Afraid was a good one: A Fraid. A Fraidy Cat. Kept him busy for almost a full minute.

Sevens had been Maxim's escape when they were young. He would count the beatings—'One, two three, four, five, six *and* seven'—and then give himself a little nod as a reward for endurance. It used to infuriate their father. Dad would give him seven more lashes and Max would just stand there, counting. Each time it happened, Bec was safe. Max took the brunt of it all. In sevens.

She'd grown past her gratitude years ago, but she was still fixed on the idea that he could protect her. Whenever she was scared, she asked him to support her. Whenever she was scared, he practised his sevens. She hated it and she felt comforted by it, both at once. Bec was bound to him by memories of their father's violence. She was the one who counted the sevens and waited for them to stop, now that they were adults.

That afternoon he started early. She kept herself grounded by thinking sympathetically of Maxim's digestive problems and the headaches and the fact that he had needed special consideration as a child. That was when he developed that mouth of his, she realised. Mum cossetted him; Dad thrashed him. He was a strange narcissistic foul-minded... protector. He was still her protector. She had taken over from Mum and he was both himself and Dad in one untidy package.

'No one's afraid of the dentist these days.' Maxim's taunts started in the car on the way over. Bec caught him admiring his elegant profile in the window and running a finger of admiration down his beautifully long jaw. Maxim's ego was impressive. Even as he admired himself, his smooth voice accused, 'You can't even get the scan done without me to hold your hand. You're eight, not twenty-eight. Why did you bother leaving home?'

She was so busy fuming about her brother's comments that she didn't find the initial tests as impossible as she had feared.

Bec was shaking, of course. She said that to herself, over and over, like a mantra, *Of course I'm shaking. I'm at the dentist. I'm not crazy, I've always been scared of the dentist.* As a child, she'd been scared to melting point, but her father had been waiting for her outside, fingering his leather belt. Her fears argued with each other until she was a shivering wreck.

Every year was the same. The night before Mum and Dad told her horror stories of screaming and teeth and monstrous forceps descending on her mouth while she was drugged and helpless. They didn't look as if they were enjoying it, ever. Their tales were matter-of-fact: these were things Bec needed to know. It was for her safety. The night before a dental appointment was full of demons. On the day itself, Dad'd make sure she didn't run away.

As soon as he was allowed, Max would go into the surgery with her and talk her through it, as he was doing now.

It had been eighteen years since she'd been to the dentist. No wonder her mouth was such a mess. No wonder the doctor had sent her here, scolded her, worried for her.

'It isn't like the old days,' the doctor had said. 'We know exactly how the mouth is linked to the rest of the body. It's dangerous to have teeth so criminally crumbling. You make that appointment now, using my phone.'

That first appointment had fortunately failed to live up to expectations. Her jaw was scanned and her samples were taken and she was told that the implants would be ready next week. Bec was ready to break into tears over the extractions. But Max stopped her crying almost before she began. 'Tears for fears,' he said.

"Extensive work" had been the promise, and extensive work was what her mouth required. Except that it had all been painless and non-invasive. Modern dentistry. Bec wanted to throw up, nonetheless. *No wonder Maxim was mocking me for being scared*, she thought, when she was finally home alone. She was still scared. She just felt stupid about her fears. About her whole life history.

She had sat in the dentist's clean office, pretending to be interested in the flower arrangement. Purples. She didn't have to be scared of purple flowers. Orchids, dyed purple. She almost relaxed as her eye traced the path the dye took through the flowers.

Then the dentist in his big black office chair said the fateful words, 'There's just one tooth that needs an old-fashioned crown. We'll do it when we inject the buds.'

'Oh good,' said Bec's brother. 'It would be a pity to waste all this grand timidity.'

Bec was confused.

'Wait!' She asked for the explanation again. Max's taunting had turned it upside down. 'Don't I have to have extractions?'

She looked at those purple orchids and she asked the dentist, more clearly this time. It seemed not. No forceps. The teeth would grow all by themselves from where they were injected, within her jaw, and, like her natural adult teeth when they had first emerged, would push the unstable and unhappy teeth out of the way. He said this in a tender baritone voice that contained an almost unholy amount of glee.

Bec wanted to turn to someone and say, 'I need a tooth fairy then,' but the only person was her brother and he was again pondering ways of making the word 'fear' into piles of fun. The dentist gave Maxim tired looks.

Bec should have gone to her appointment alone. She knew that. But she couldn't bring herself to. She wanted to apologise on the way out, for her brother being her brother. *He loves me, really*, she consoled herself. Somewhere deep down. *Besides, he came with me, didn't he? And he's coming again next week.*

I'm not going to think about next week's appointment, she decided that night. *It's all going to be too much. Injections for anaesthetic and injections for toothbuds and drilling and everything horrid. A tooth stripped naked and ground down. Maxim is coming to distract me.* He had promised before she could ask. Their father had made them interdependent in the unhappiest ways. *Stupid of me not to refuse him outright. Stupid of me to be scared. No one's scared of the dentist anymore. No one except me.*

If Max and the dentist exchange more meaningful looks, I think I shall die.

Max thinks he's being funny. I've no idea what the dentist thinks. I don't even know what his name is.

Max had taken the card with the appointment written on it. 'If you're going to act like a baby,' he said, 'I'll just take charge of this.' The humiliation was almost too much.

Bec sat in the old-fashioned long dental chair and the dentist tuned it so that she'd be comfortable. Its apparent age scared her. She kept envisaging a big hairy bloke looking over her, with forceps clenched in his beefy right hand. The dentist wasn't big, he wasn't hairy, and the chair wasn't so old-fashioned, she realised, for it was tuned from a tiny console on the dentist's own chair. And he was left-handed.

When the dentist was certain she could see the screen a metre and a half away, and that she was at the right angle for evil operations on her poor mouth, he nodded to himself briefly and then gave her a sweet smile. He hadn't smiled at all sweetly the other day.

Or if he had, she'd been too busy watching those orchids.

'We're ready,' he said. 'D'you want to see what your teeth will look like?'

'You can't know,' said Maxim, reminding everyone he was there. 'They're not even grown yet. You can't know what they'll look like.'

'If we can't know what they'll look like then we'll find out. If she doesn't like it, she'll come back, and I'll fix them, pronto and painless,' the dentist corrected him, mildly. 'I offer this every time, but no one ever needs it. The new techniques are rather effective. I've never had a patient who hasn't had perfect replacement teeth within two weeks. Sometimes a crown has to be adjusted a little, but replacement teeth, never. Our little vat grows those babies miraculously.'

'It's not natural,' said Maxim.

Bec's mind turned to vats of artificial meat, to vats of bacteria decomposing rubbish, to vats of… she said the first thing that came into her mouth, to turn off those images.

'I'd like to see.'

It wasn't such a bad thing to say, after all. Maybe if she saw the display of her teeth-to-be, then her brother would turn the flat comment on her later, rather than sooner. The whole way into the surgery she'd suffered his wit and really, she didn't want more of it. That short peace had been such a blessing. The sooner his wit was finished for the day, the better.

Technowizardry reduced Max for about a minute. The teeth-*in-potentia* fashion-paraded across the screen singly, then lined up dutifully within the image of Bec's mouth.

'Wouldn't it have been easier to replace all my teeth?' Bec asked, tentatively. There must be a reason and she didn't want to face the crown. 'Like they used to take them all out and give a young woman a complete set of false teeth for her twenty-first?' Bec knew all the stories of toothy horror.

'Oh God,' said the dentist. 'I'd forgotten that. Barbarous practice.' Maybe this was not a forceps dentist. Maybe forceps dentists didn't exist anymore.

'It wouldn't be as expensive if you had a complete fix,' Max scoffed. 'The whole mouth. All your teeth. That one crown costs more than seven toothbuds.' Max had always been good at arithmetic.

The dentist raised an eyebrow in Bec's direction and ignored Maxim utterly.

'The reason we don't replace everything is because we prefer to save your existing teeth where we can and because the bone—'

'But,' Max interrupted before the dentist could finish, 'that tooth's only got a few more years and the new teeth are perfect. You said so.' He sounded triumphant, his voice a trumpet turning the music back on itself.

'Crowns have greater stability and are set on the patient's own teeth. If the patient has a strong desire to have them replaced, we will oblige, but reluctantly.'

We will oblige. The dentist was making a point. He talked to Bec, but his face was carefully tilted to show that the statement was as much for Max.

Bec demurred. 'I just want the teeth you've already worked out.'

She didn't want to be here and she didn't want it to hurt, but she trusted the dentist's judgement. He had, after all, a very good reputation. Also, crowns didn't have to grow in her jawline—she would be able to eat immediately, to smile immediately and, most importantly, to be pain-free immediately. And her doctor would give her the all clear and she could return to normal life. She could forget dentists for another eighteen years.

That was all she wanted, to have the threat of heart problems lifted and to have the headaches gone and to be herself again. *This* was why she had braved the white cubicle with its carefully manipulable chair and its screen of teeth on parade.

'Do the teeth do a song and dance?' She indicated the screen.

The dentist smiled his sweet smile. 'How did you guess? My assistant programmed it. Whenever things are slow, she fiddles with it. Watch.' And they all watched Bec's teeth sing and dance to "Cry Me a River".

'What are the words for, karaoke night?' Maxim's tone was scathing. He didn't approve of the levity of others.

'Of course,' the dentist said. 'Once a month. On Thursdays. I always sing Aretha Franklin songs.'

He was so obviously pleased about this that Maxim's comment sounded nastier than he'd intended. Not that he'd intended to be nice. To Bec it sounded as if her brother was rather viciously attacking a sweet-tempered man in a white coat. He was attacking a friendly smile and a slightly daft sense of humour.

It made Bec wonder. Was the dentist really as charming as he sounded? For, if he were clever, he could have made Max look bad, quite intentionally. Bec wanted to think about it. She wanted a long, placid time. There wouldn't be one.

The karaoke had been the last straw for Max. Bec sighed. She knew what was coming next. The signs were all there: the tightening around the mouth, the slight squint in the eyes, the sharpening of the voice. It would take a moment to emerge, however.

'And now,' the dentist said, pre-empting Max, 'let's get to work. If you're okay with your teeth, I'll send them for final prep.'

Bec nodded and the dentist pressed a button.

'They're gone,' he said. 'Watch.'

The tune changed and the teeth sang and danced 'so long' and 'farewell' and '*auf wiedersehen*' and 'goodbye' and drifted off the screen.

'I'll pick them up from the bath when we're ready,' the dentist said.

Why didn't he have a nametag? Why didn't she look at his name on the email when she'd booked? Why hadn't she asked when the DNA sequencing was done? He was full of personality and yet was just 'the dentist'. It was stupid. Bec hated herself.

'Where's the bath?' Maxim asked. 'Next to the toilets?'

'In the back office.' This young man was determined not to get offended. Bec wanted to fall in love with him, just for a moment. 'Next to the machine that carves out the crowns. I love that machine.' The dentist's eyes were smitten. 'The diamond drill is my favourite. I could watch it for hours. It whittles the perfect crown in less than ten minutes. A decade ago it was fifteen minutes. A decade before that we had to send it out to the technician and it took two weeks.'

'Murderers could use it to carve bones and get rid of evidence.' Max had obviously been kind long enough. *It's probably retribution. No one needs that stuff anymore,* Maxim had told her, when she had explained the dental situation. *But I'll stand by you. I always do.* He always said he did. And he sometimes he actually did.

Other peoples' brothers were worse, Bec reflected. Often worse, anyhow. Or maybe she just thought they were worse. If she didn't, she'd never talk to her own brother ever again.

'Is it genetic?' asked Bec. 'I mean, the work my teeth need?'

Maxim had an answer before the dentist could speak. 'Quite probably. Thank God I get my face from the other side of the family,' and he admired his long jawline in the window opposite.

It was such a typical thing for Max to do: find the nearest reflection and pose. Sometimes Bec wanted to punch his elegant jaw, or maybe angle her fist towards his nose. Right now, though, she needed him. She was terrified of the procedure and Maxim was her support and her protection. Also, he was her brother and he owed her. Reflected in the window next to Max was the dentist's face. He was looking at Maxim's jawline and he was smiling. It wasn't the sweet smile of earlier.

Now it was down to business. Bec was injected. The injection hurt and she whimpered. Her whole jaw hurt for a minute and then her face went gradually numb. Then the drilling started. The whine of the high-speed drill made her wince, but she knew that this was the memory of early pain: she couldn't feel anything. It still hurt. Her hands clenched into fists and the dentist was busy getting rid of the antiquated filling and so Maxim had the floor and she had no choice but to listen. This is when it became obvious, far too late, why Maxim had chosen to come with her. Playing with words had been just a diversion: now he was warmed up.

He wanted her in a position where she couldn't reply, where she couldn't even nod. She hated the whine of the drill and had only just got past the needle without screaming and Maxim's voice pounded, pounded, pounded in her ear, telling her things she shouldn't, didn't ever want to hear. He told her that she had deserved it when Mum and Dad stopped speaking to her and that she had demanded a life alone by the way she failed to successfully manage her life. He told her what a failure she was and that the colour of her hair was fake. He told her all her fears, for he knew them better than anyone.

The dentist asked him to stop talking once, twice, three times.

Each time, Max took a moment's respite then started up again. Bec wished the dentist would send Max to the waiting room. Then she didn't, for she was scared: there was a drill in her mouth. Old family habits of support held true, even when her brother was being his impossible self.

Max told her that he was repossessing his television from her. He told her that she would never get a boyfriend again. He said that her ex had been forced out of their lives by her own laziness. He told her things about her body that she knew were not true, but had to believe for here they were, reinforced by the sound of that drill. He told her and told her and told her and it was lies and she knew it but she didn't know it, because it felt like the truth, there in the place of her worst fears. She listened and listened and wept inside.

'Do you want to get rid of him?' the dentist whispered, when Max excused himself for a toilet break.

'Yes. No. I can't.'

'You're still scared of me?' His voice was sweet and up close his hair had greying tufts sticking out at irregular angles. She wanted to pat those curls and the scraps of grey and say, *It's all right*. Except it wasn't.

'Not you. Of forceps. Of pain. Of... everything.'

'The worst's over,' he said. 'That's all the pain there will be. I promise not to use forceps.'

'My last dentist used forceps and left bits of tooth behind. I stopped going to the dentist. I had such nightmares.'

'None.'

'And drilling?'

'A bit of final shaping to the crown. Not on your tooth at all.'

'I still need my brother,' Bec whispered, ashamed. Her family had left her such a legacy.

'Of course. The science changes things, but we have to give ourselves time to adapt to those changes.'

'You mean it'll fade? I won't be so scared?'

'Give yourself permission not to be frightened,' he suggested. 'See what happens.'

And then Max came back and the assistant brought the new cap in from its diamond drilling adventures and it all started again. This time, it was different. Max's mouth spewed vileness and Bec still wept inside, but a part of her was objective. A small corner of her soul listened and looked and that part of her wondered, 'Can it change?'

When Max finally ran out of words, the dentist told her to rinse.

'That wasn't so bad, was it?' said Maxim. 'Nothing like family to hold your hand when you're scared.'

'I never want you near me again.' Bec was not loud, but she was clear.

'What about next time you need your teeth fixed?'

'I'll be scared. Not such a big deal, being scared. I can handle it.'

The dentist nodded, his nice smile all gone. He looked as if he were contemplating something. Or tasting something.

Maxim stopped to admire his elegant jawline just one more time on the way out. He was impervious to the swarm of nastiness that had emerged from his own mouth. It was as if he had whispered it to her privately, in a dream.

The dentist noticed his gaze and spoke directly to Maxim. 'You have a Hapsburg jaw,' he said. 'You really should get that asymmetry looked at. Philip II of Spain had it.'

'A bit of attention won't go astray,' Maxim admitted. He looked at his face in the window again, admiring the jaw of the Holy Roman Emperors.

'I'll write you a referral.'

'A referral?' Maxim's superiority showed. He smiled.

'What sort of treatment is it?' Bec asked, worried. She knew that the actual dentistry wasn't the problem, it was her brother. Maybe she was doomed to worry about everything, just as she was doomed to assume the worst from everything Max said. She'd been saying this to herself for most of her life and the moment of truth had been just that. Bec admitted though that she treasured that clear moment when she finally saw her brother's words as an evil swarm, infesting the clean white dental surgery.

'It's a hospital visit,' the dentist explained. 'Your jaw will have to be broken and reset and then adjusted gradually. It takes months. Very painful. Like braces, but rather worse.'

'What about the wonders of modern science? Don't I get DNA testing and machine scans?'

'Quite possibly, but that's to check things. It's not the treatment. Realigning your jawline to make it functional is also very much the wonder of modern science, you know. The original Hapsburgs couldn't eat properly and had perpetual indigestion and bad breath,' the dentist said with mild relish. 'Every day it will get a bit worse. Or you could have the operation and adjustment. It may take a long time and be very painful, but it'll be fixed. At least you understand pain,' the dentist added thoughtfully.

Two faces turned towards him. Maxim's was tight and compressed. Men in white coats were supposed to be part of the furniture: they weren't supposed to notice, and they especially weren't supposed to demonstrate sarcasm. And Bec, Bec at that moment lost her fear of dentistry entirely.

It was never the pain that had scared her, it was the inhumanity. It was her father with his soulless words and propensity for violence. This new dentist of hers was proving himself very, very human. The very, very human dentist raised an eyebrow at her and said, 'Come back in two weeks, just for a check.'

'Okay,' said Bec. She took a deep breath. She wreaked revenge. 'Maxim, I'll hold your hand when you go to hospital to get your jaw broken. I'll be your support and your strength.'

The white chamber seemed suddenly empty of noise.

'Would you care to go to dinner with me next Thursday?' the dentist asked Bec.

'I'd be delighted,' Bec answered, dignified. 'I hope it means I get to sing.'

'All the Aretha Franklin is mine,' the dentist warned her.

'I'll remember that. I might sing seven songs, to make up.' And Bec, for the first time ever, smiled in a dental surgery.

Someone's Daughter

It starts with me. Everything always starts with me. My beloved says so, for I am black and comely and my breath reminds him of myrrh or spikenard, if only he could remember which. 'Sorry, my dear, but I always confuse the Song of Songs with some hymn or other.' Before me, he says, it was a group of university bods, digging up the soil. I made it all human, he says. I made it mean something.

Except it's not my story. So it doesn't start with me. It doesn't end with me. It just goes through me. It gives me indigestion as it goes through me, like very bad wind, but one day soon it will be finished, and I will feel a great deal better. I will remember everything, even the dark. I may even be able to tell the tales I was born to tell. You will have the tale I have to tell and then you can have an echo of my evil breeze. That's what comes next. Sharing the pain. The next step for me may be death. If it is, I won't be the first. Something in me is resigned. Something else in me is angry. I myself am absent unless I concentrate carefully and close my mind against the wind. I cannot always take it seriously.

But where does it start? I mean, what triggered this story? Can I tell it as if I were my old self, hard and flip and joyously pragmatic, excited about life, love and the past? Or will the wind rip it away from me before I can finish? I am better than the winds of time and I am better than the night, and stronger, and I shall tell my story, right through to the end.

It starts with a grave.

This grave was a big discovery. No disputing it. It wasn't the bones of Richard III and his scoliosis, but it was just as good. 'A queen's body,' they announced. Not Christian, judging not only from the grave goods (which were mostly terribly Anglo-Saxon) but from the single line in the sole anonymous chronicle that recorded it and from an abbreviated Gildas reference. (I distrust Gildas, but then, he was misogynist and would have distrusted me back.) Anonymous Monk lived near here, but his chronicle went to London when the monasteries were dissolved. Where the entries differ from the other chronicles of the day, they demonstrate a man after my own heart: he made his loves and hates known, very clearly. The historians say that he was local. All his personal comments relate to known local figures so there appears to be no doubt that this woman was one such.

'She is dead,' said the chronicle, 'of plague. God is triumphant. God is just.' Gildas listed her as one of the evil rulers. It wasn't an interesting mention.

The grave goods, in fact, were better than Richard's (which were, to be truthful, non-existent).

The grave goods were astonishing, even more astonishing than finding the body of another ruler Anonymous Monk had hated. He was such a good hater.

There was nothing quite like this burial. It was rare and it was special and even as the top layer of soil came off, it appeared to be very rich. It had been left alone for almost fifteen hundred years.

There were local superstitions about the grave. Every couple of days a local would come forth and inform us of this. They were having us on. They would admit it, each night when we joined them for drinks. There were no stories. There were no superstitions. But someone else would come down two days later and inform us of the evil contained within this mound.

'It kills babies,' one middle-aged man informed us, significantly, his hands in the pocket of his suit, hidden from the wind. 'And murders their mothers.'

'You ought to be a peasant,' my boss said. 'Offering us up superstitions on a platter. And don't you live just down the road? Isn't your youngest in school with my oldest?' We're an inbred society, us university archaeologists. Everything and everyone is round the corner.

'My ancestors were good yeoman stock,' he volunteered. 'And yes, I do, and yes, they are.'

'That's what everyone says about their ancestors. 'Good yeoman stock',' she retorted. 'There were a lot of yeomen in this area.'

'Only one' —the local gave up on seriousness— 'but he got around.' He joined us at the pub that evening, along with everyone else, and we didn't hear anything more about infant mortality.

An hour. I defeated the wind for an hour.

During those early stages we were more thorough even than we needed to be. The site was too unexpected and far too rich. The weather held well enough and we retrieved artefact after artefact. As each was carefully extracted and dealt with, we slowed down and became more careful. There were too many anomalies in the grave goods. There was also something about the bones, though no-one was saying what, and they had already been hustled into the lab.

Over and over, we checked everything. We had to. No other female leader was mentioned in Gildas. No other burial was able to be identified with that one line in a local chronicle: 'She is dead,' said the chronicle, 'of plague. God is triumphant. God is just.' God is just, but his followers buried this woman with fine ceramic ware, imported.

That single line, plus Gildas and the grave goods, pointed clearly to a sixth-century burial. Possibly mid-century. And this time, I lost three-quarters of my hour to darkness. My true love feels he can prevail by reciting psalms. I measure my mind's strength against the wind by my heart's religion. When my love talks about lying down in green pastures and runs his sentences together until they are impossibly long, I cackle hysterically and think of that woman, lying down under green pastures, surrounded by wealth. We try cooking instead.

The ceramic bowls alone—imported from North Africa—made the grave goods an archaeologist's dream. They were extraordinarily fine and contained traces (in some instances, more than traces) of their contents. We were bubbling with excitement but exploring the innards of bowls was something for down the track. There was so much to occupy us. Every day we found more goods. There were exquisite beads of amethyst and Baltic amber. There was enough glass and gold to pay for six armies. Clothes and cloth, shattered by time, mere scraps clinging to the backs of brooches and baubles, waiting to be interpreted into garments by a textiles expert. There was metalwork. More pots. More glass jars. These also had echoes of the resins they had once held, fragrances spent a millennium and a half before. Myrrh, perhaps, or spikenard. We didn't yet know.

The brilliance of the finds obscured the importance of the iron chest. We saw it early, but left it in the ground for later as it looked like nothing more than a big metal lump. We worked around it, extracting the beautiful and the rare and the fragile. I handled that corner of the trench and so I was the one who cleared the space around it. Just a simple iron chest. I call it a simple iron chest, but a chest made of iron is rare and precious, it was just overshadowed initially. It wasn't very big. Well-made, but not fitting comfortably with the luxury of the rest of the grave.

I carefully cleaned the outside of that chest and tried to lever it open. That was surprising. The tight iron covering had protected its contents superbly. I could see one large gold cube sitting on top of others and there were spindles and whorls and the stuff of daily life filling the space between them. I carefully closed the lid again, for the iron box and its contents had to wait for its time, but one thing was obvious: the gold box on the top was not simply made of beaten metal—it was the exterior of some sort of mechanism. There was a key sitting on it, and when I turned it (which was wrong of me, but I wasn't the only one tempted) there was a whirring sound. This was extraordinary. A fifteen-centimetre gold cube, with a beautifully embossed exterior, with a keyhole and some kind of internal mechanism. And it was still *in situ*. Further exploration was just not possible. Telephone calls were made. Three hours later, when the site closed for the night, there were watchmen watching.

Christmas carols work delightfully at keeping the wind outside my mind and the dark from invading. Twelve watchers watching, eleven canons singing, ten ladies laughing, nine babies buried, eight whorls a-whirling, seven lords a-loving, six vicars praying, five gold rings.

The pub that night had one small but noisy table. It kept being shushed, for everyone else wanted to watch the jubilee concert.

'An Anglo-Saxon Antikythera mechanism!' exclaimed a postgraduate volunteer.

'Don't get too excited,' warned her supervisor. 'They're almost certainly boxes. Unheard-of technologies in Anglo-Saxon England are not likely.' The boss was confined to non-alcoholic drinks because of her pregnancy, and was sour as a result.

'I want to prove that our ancestors had amazing technologies that have been forgotten.'

'Go on wanting,' retorted the professor. 'Just don't try to make a career of it.'

That postgraduate volunteer was me, not yet with wind. I'd been volunteered by my supervisor (who I called 'the boss', even though the professor was really the boss: their real names were Smith and Smith, so we all avoided that, my boss and the prof, and they were the whole of management) and we were both wildly excited. My yearning and wistful beauty (or maybe the drinks I bought management) meant I was assigned to the boxes as junior staff (I had barely enough conservation experience) that night. I'd been forgiven my transgression. I had to wait, however. First, there was so much else to do. The box had been buried deep and around it there was much to be done before the box could be carefully broached again.

Each find had to be dealt with properly. Antikythera or not, due sequence couldn't be shirked. If due sequence was shirked (as I'd been reminded, several times), then finds would perish, and our understanding of the past would crumble and rust and decay as we observed. Like my mind, now, except that I'm winning. The darkness is safe, but I will not go there.

'When we get a bit further,' the boss promised, 'you get next look inside.' In the meantime, the box had been lifted out of its position in the grave and was waiting in the conservation lab.

There were more breaks in proceedings where we met and mingled with the locals. I was mingling with a local in the churchyard, which was maybe fifty metres from our site and very convenient.

'Evil,' the pastor said to me, very matter-of-factly. 'Don't let it worry you, she is definitely dead. She hurt us then, can't hurt us now.' With no definite intent on our part, we were in the graveyard, standing underneath the yew. He was leaning on a nice tomb, eighteenth century, judging by the winged death's head. The winged death's head was cute, but the pastor was cuter.

'Some of my ancestors come from around here,' I admitted. 'It's like closing a loop.'

'This isn't a horror novel,' he said, 'But if you're from around here, we'll forgive you the accent and see you in church on Sunday.'

'In your dreams,' I said.

The wind rustled the yew.

As we went our respective ways, he called after me, 'Then how about dinner tonight?'

That was as loud as it got. The local cleric shouting a dinner invitation.

The media would have gone wild over this grave from a time ancient and unknown, which had such a wicked reputation (though no one would tell me what the reputation was, not even my cute young man from the graveyard, which made me think that it was more Aunt Ada Doom than anything actually wrong with the green mound we were digging into) but none of our lords and masters from the university were certain how to handle it. They were paying for guards. They didn't want looting. They didn't want the gaping maws of tourists. Mostly, however, they didn't want the unwilling American couple who had recently bought the old rectory to revoke their permission to dig. 'It creeps me out,' the woman told anyone who would listen. 'I'm not going near it.' The media was not informed of any of this.

We all put our material in and it disappeared into the system, to be thrown out again as scraps of official documentation. Those scraps became our first public report. I didn't mind if it said more about the general location and contexts than about what we had found. It referred to Gildas and the chronicle, but didn't quote, which was a bit unusual. I didn't care, however. The longer the dig lasted, the more time I'd spend with the man next door.

We hadn't opened the boxes yet. There was still too much work to be done and we were so few people and had to observe due processes lest the sky fall. So there was much cataloguing and drawing and cleaning and preserving and stabilising and entering into databases and photographing and matching pieces and identifying and simply working through each shard one by one. When we dug our first trench, we thought that our team was a miniature horde. We'd all seen quick and dirty jobs where only one or two people had to get out a report within a fortnight and then the whole thing was done. This was the stuff of modern archaeology. Private sector work. But we were not the private sector. We had the entire summer, and significant segments of the seasons beyond. We put in long days to get the basics finished within the time frame, even so. The university administration fretted at us the whole slow path, as they always did.

The body was still being dealt with offsite. None of us knew what was happening with it. I had the promise of opening a box but couldn't actually get near it. I took out my impatience at the pub, in drinks, and spent a lot more time in the graveyard. Those days were all about dirt and forms and the slowness of progress.

Word came back about the body before we'd finished. Our bone people are extraordinarily good.

Our queen had apparently not died from the plague as was recorded by that holy monk from the sixth century. The bones showed clear signs of abuse. There were knife marks and breaks and indents and hollows and localised shattering. Our queen (in full adulthood, still of childbearing years) had been beaten and stabbed and her bones were broken until she died of the trauma. Our nameless woman had been murdered. For being a ruler, the historians suggest. For not being male. As punishment for whatever had gone wrong, whether it was the plague or the harvest failure. Everyone knew that Gildas wrote about a time of terrible trouble for Britain: it was still shocking to see the mess the murderers had made of this woman's skeleton.

The grave goods made no sense alongside the violence. Love? Appeasement? Whatever the reason, she had died a horrible death. We had printouts of the photos taken of her ruined frame and we took them to the pub and we wept over them, maudlin with beer and memory. Someone left those printouts on the pub table, and I stole them.

We created a story for her, my pastor and I, that evening, holed up with just the photographs and a big bed. We dreamed of what it might have been like to be this one little queen in the middle of nowhere and the middle of no-time. This battered and knifed and tortured and bedamned woman with the rich burial goods. This non-Christian.

I get indigestion just thinking about the murder. It's as if I can feel a thin iron knife sliding in between my ribs and then the butt of it crashing down upon my ribcage. The wind; the indigestion; the murder: they are one.

Since that evening in the pub, no one has talked about the bones offsite. Before then, we didn't talk about the burial goods, or even the dig. Just something we were doing to make our CVs look good, we said, if prodded. We all had different reasons for not talking about such a big find. The boss and the boss's boss didn't know if it would make or break careers, for instance. Me, I'm the one who had first seen the iron box. I wanted my time with it. Besides, I had distractions.

Even so, we were slow in reaching the iron chest. It would take maybe two years to properly document the other finds, so we had an excuse for prioritising. There was something about that whirring sound that was disconcerting, however. Clockwork in an Anglo-Saxon site was unheard of. I think we didn't want to find out that we had been subject to a clever and expensive fraud. We told ourselves that we were establishing the truth of the grave before we worried about the one object that absolutely didn't fit.

Next week, they would say, *we'll be able to finally start on the box. To talk about the dig. All of it will happen at once.* Those few days were difficult. Inside, I was a ferment of impatience. Outside, I was an articulate university student, with breath that apparently smelled like church incense.

'Come to a service,' he suggested.

'Latin,' I replied, every time. 'If I'm going to celebrate a God in which I don't believe, it has to be in Latin.'

The big iron box was still waiting back at the conservation lab. No one was sure of its condition. And so the decision was that I would open it. Finally. And count those golden boxes again. And see what else it hid. Finally.

I felt something strange about the boxes from the moment I was allowed to lift that iron lid and cautiously take out one of my glorious treasures. The boss took one look and told me to put it back. The proportions were unsettling in the artificial light. It was as if they were designed by a perverse mind. It measured as a cube, but it looked warped.

'Is there just the one?' She covered the tension with a question to which she knew the answer. Neither of us wanted to draw that box.

'Three. Just to confirm, officially. Ouch.' I'd stabbed my thumb against something, putting the golden casket back.

'Don't go all Sleeping Beauty on me.' The boss found me amusing. 'Report it as you find it—I'm taking notes.'

'A spindle,' I said, peering into the dark, everyone else still shining torches uselessly around my head. 'It's sharper than other spindles I've encountered. Mind you, those other spindles were modern. I've never had close encounter with an ancient spindle before.' I sucked my thumb for a moment.

'I know the spindle. I saw it. Along with spare whorls underneath. Symbolic, I would guess, in a female burial. Extraordinary that the wood has survived. Quite possibly unique.'

'Oh,' said I, feeling stupid. 'That's why you made the Sleeping Beauty comment.'

'You are wise among postgrads. Now, is that another box I see?'

'Two more. They're a matched set. I noticed that when we opened it the first time. The craftsmanship! They're all hammered gold and outside my league. I wonder if the other two are also Antikythera things?' Strange mechanisms. That was what I had found unsettling. The oddness of an unknown technology. Something shuddered inside me then I relaxed. I moved over to let the boss in. She, too, pricked her finger with the spindle and we made more Sleeping Beauty jokes.

The next day, the boss wasn't there. The ambulance had taken her, just after we closed the site for the night. It was a miscarriage. In this day and age of great science, both of them died. We were informed when we turned up for work the next morning. I still don't believe it. I still look for her around the corner, drinking takeaway coffee and eating yet another of the vile cakes she loved. The site was closed a day for mourning. Only a day. We were back the day after and that night we drank a toast in the pub to our favourite academic.

Someone said, when we were properly maudlin and had lost all sense of propriety, that the baby was alive. It was being kept quiet. The baby of my mentor. I wanted to go visit. I tried anyway. I'm not next of kin, but I wanted to try, at least. Armed guards stopped me going in.

That was just plain stupid. I decided the baby was a rumour based on misery and moved on. Both my old friend and my to-be friend had died and I shut my mind off from it.

Maybe I moved on. Or maybe it was the wind swirling. I know it was the wind for I know when it started blowing. I'm not saying. I'm not writing it down. It's real if I say it directly and today I would rather it were unreal. Tomorrow, I may find courage.

We kept digging. After a week, we all put down our tools and put on our best dark clothes and went to farewell the boss properly, in the graveyard next door (for she had lived locally). That was somehow fitting. The funeral wasn't a farewell, though. It felt wrong. There were too many strangers. The professor and I took one look at all these strangers and at the way they wore suits and resolved to stick together.

After the ceremony, we were joined by the ceremonial person himself. The vicar was in confessional mood and felt impelled to tell the professor many secrets.

'We married,' he said. The boss had heralded our new life before she died and gave my vicar and myself a fine set of eighteenth-century dishes for our wedding. There was no understanding her death. At dinner after the event, she had complained of indigestion and sometimes her eyes looked unfocussed, as if she were seeing behind the wind.

'Who marries the marry-er?' The professor knew everything but asked anyway. We all do this. We spend so much time together that we have the same habits. My poor love, who sees echoes of me everywhere.

'The registry office,' my Solomon said, enjoying the irony. Irony is a major addiction of his, along with misquoting the Old Testament. 'We'll do a church wedding when I've convinced my love of the existence of God, which may not be in this lifetime.'

'I believe in little green men,' I suggested helpfully. He gave me a hug.

We were being crowded by the unknowns. I didn't want to share private conversations with men who enjoyed wearing black suits unless I was marrying them, I joked, and the three of us left.

The next day I noticed one of the men who found suits too comfortable ostentatiously hiding behind a newspaper.

'Too many movies,' I told myself and then worried. What if it was something the boss knew? What had killed the boss? Did they think I knew something too? Movie mania zapped me. Or maybe the black had reached into my brain. I was caught in a moment where life wasn't quite real, where a simple phone call was an impossible task. My true love and I read Bede of an evening, for we were an old couple. No more pictures of battered bones in our bed: just ourselves and perhaps an echo of the wind. I should have settled, but I did not.

I acted like someone in a bad archaeological film. I dressed in black. I stole into the offices by night and downloaded all the files. When I got them home, I sat up all night, scrolling through, trying to find out what the suits were about. I should stop calling them suits. Mostly they wore jeans. They just behaved as if they were wearing black suits and were about to tamper with our minds and change reality. I need to stop watching those movies.

Most of the files reflected exactly what I knew. I drooled over the grave goods again. The boxes had been checked in the lab and contained mechanisms, but no one could work out what they did. I felt cheated; my boxes had been examined without me.

What rocked me was that they had found DNA. They had already run checks on it and done so with extraordinary speed. The face had not even been reconstructed and they had analysed her DNA.

In the DNA file was a reference to another file. A locked one. The idiots who locked it had used the boss's name as their password.

DNA testing shows that the buried woman was not entirely human.

They have it on all the science fiction shows; aliens who are so advanced that they can create cuckoo children.

The files suggested a trigger. Something that changed receptive genes, genes with the right marker. Intentional epigenetics. How to hide a race inside another race.

The file suggested that the outcomes were unreliable. They didn't know how the trigger had operated. The only case they had, however, was the boss. Who had died. The cause of death was her become-alien baby. Her body couldn't handle it. Babies were already alien, I thought, and I lost an hour to the wind and to the dark. Thank God I was home at the time. The only hurt done was to my computer, which had been running on battery. I plugged it in and returned to the locked file. The file that described sleeping alien genes.

I'm reading words I don't understand. Epigenetics is the worst of them. I'm throwing those words around as if they mean something. They're just wind. Wind blowing through my mind. My mind doesn't always operate the way it used to.

That damned spindle. Sleeping Beauty. Stories came from somewhere. Of course, they murdered the woman who changed their babies into something else. But what? What did the babies become? Will we find a mass grave near here? All the little children? Is the worst of the past still to come?

I was almost definitely not going to die (since I was still alive), but it wasn't just about me.

I felt stupid doing it, but I went to one of my scientist friends and got them drunk. I took the boss's DNA and the dead queen's DNA (both on the files I had lifted) and I also hauled up that DNA test we did as a class exercise when we were undergrads ('Where do humans come from?' we'd been told to ask. 'How many different sources are there?').

My friend compared them. It took him six months and dinted my alcohol budget, but he compared them. By the time he was finished, I was done with the doctorate, which was just as well. No longer a postgraduate: I was a married archaeologist in search of employ.

'You're all related,' he said.

'That's unexpected,' I said, wondering how I'd missed the blue-eye gene.

'Not at all. Common ancestors.'

'Anything… strange?'

'I have no idea. We don't know the half of what's in us yet.'

I am willing to lay odds that my DNA has the markers that hers has. That alien ancient queen. That murdered body with the burial so fine. One of the strange mechanisms in the box recognised me, I thought, for that is what the classified scientists had thought, in their locked file. It probably also recognised that I was pregnant. Only barely pregnant, then. Very, very pregnant now. Next week, I shall be a mother.

Initially, I believed the reports I had copied, that the strange boxed mechanism was to blame. Now, I think it was the spindle. I suspect that everything in the iron chest had its own mechanisms; some were more cunningly hidden than others. They had all been buried out of reach. In iron. We had copied Pandora, woken Sleeping Beauty. We had no idea. And now my mind is here and my mind is there and my mind is everywhere the wind blows.

I get indigestion thinking about the consequences. No nausea. No symptoms of pregnancy except my mind-drift. It killed my boss but it can't kill me. Won't kill me. I don't know why. I should ask, except the thinker inside me is cosseted to sleep when I try: we don't want to know. And besides, all we have is a set of assumptions based on a quick reading of data by a small group of young people who really don't know what they're doing. If the pair of us thought the professors knew any more than us, then we would surrender to them, give them my body and my child for tests in the interstices when the wind isn't blowing.

I can't do it alone. Or even as part of a couple.

I tried. I was waiting to buy a ticket to catch the train to go London to turn myself in when my mind was vacant and happy and windswept. I don't remember the windswept. I remember waking up on the pier at Brighton, wondering why the waves were so small and wondering why the waves were an odd colour and wondering what was wrong. Half-aware, I thought it was the wrong Brighton. Now I realise that it was the wrong planet.

Maybe the murdered woman was like me, a product of that spindle. Maybe my baby will be mostly human.

Himself is reassuring, but then, Himself has God on his side. I find myself envying him that God.

In our lighter moods, my beloved and I argue for green skin. We can't argue the baby away. I ached over it, but he was firm: we must face this birth. He wanted to face it with stoicism and to bring the baby up as if nothing was happening, as if our tiny one wasn't the vanguard of ancient change. I was firm: I can't keep the story from the world. And so we are the guardians of the first part of humanity's future. God help us.

I talk about the wind, but inside I still feel the slithering knife and see the bones of the dead queen, spread like refuse over our fine double bed.

My Life—Briefly

I started reading a fairy story a few minutes ago. I had to put it down immediately because it began "Once upon a time".

It struck me suddenly that "Once upon a time" is a charming way to start a story, but that it is not really the way I would start my life history. My favourite description of these matters for a long time was "relative"—I age like almost anyone (there must be people who don't age, but I have not yet met them, a joy in store), I just do not age in the same perceived timeframe, and I seem to jump back and forth in the most egregiously strange manner from five to fifty and down to five again in a single day. This life experience has warped me, naturally.

Sometimes I think my life is like a lived version of Tristram Shandy's, with all the tidy chronological recounting happening in the nine months before my birth. It certainly has not been chronological since then, and I seem to have lost the manner of even thinking in a neatly linear fashion because, as my mother says, 'If you do not live lineally, why think lineally,' which is not really a reassuring thought. My story is too diffuse and diverse for anything that makes sense in a normal manner. And my life story has never really had a "once"—a key date when you could say it started—or a "time" because a specific location in the space-time continuum is something I have never really fixated on (by fixated on, I mean fretted about unduly, since it was patently lacking). I envied Dr Who the assumed personal linearity of his TARDIS in the odd periods when I met his character on TV. And I also envied a storyline that must have developed over time, but which I couldn't see because, frankly, I never saw more than an episode or two before warping off into my own strangely multidimensional existence. Nothing has so far adequately explained how I can still be human and still speak English. Not even Dr Who.

Maybe there are ways of picking up culture without that external sequentiality? This is something I must consider a bit more because it really does imply I have personal sequentiality and development; I just assumed that the personal stuff went out the door with the external stuff (if I look five, surely I am five). Perhaps my thinking on this is just plain wrong, and I do live lineally, just not in the same manner as everyone else.

Perhaps I need to fixate on time a little more than I have. Sorting out what the hell time is and how it affects me has never really been something I understood. Right now, this bugs the hell out of me.

Am I in time-space adolescence? Or am I just annoyed by "Once upon a time"?

Impractical Magic

The invocation faded into the still air. Nothing happened.

Thank God the children were out and had not been party to this *glorious* attempt at summoning a demon. Maybe it was Zoë who had all the magic and her mother was just a hiccup in the family tradition? Judith let her tension whoosh out in a sigh: the test had failed.

'Next time you don't quite believe something is real,' she scolded herself, 'don't bloody well bother trying to prove it.'

She walked downstairs weightily and decided she needed a cup of tea to cure exhaustion. And chocolate. Lots and lots of chocolate. Lots and lots and lots, as twelve-year-old Zoë would say.

In the kitchen, sitting at the table, drinking her best coffee (which had been squiggled away where the children couldn't get to it), was a tall, dark and handsome man. Very tall, very dark and spectacularly handsome.

Judith sighed again. It was the day of the clichés. He rose to greet her, and Judith amended her thoughts as her neck tilted upwards. Very, very tall. Too tall. And not a man. His eyes were deep red and dangerous.

'Ashmodai?' she ventured, cautiously. 'Did I summon you?'

'You did,' answered the King of Demons, his voice rich with nuance and echo. 'You have called me forth from the interminable horror of my dank captivity.'

'Why is captivity always dank?' Judith asked, choosing to ignore his eyes. 'And why didn't you come upstairs when I called, damn your little toe?'

'My little toe is already damned, according to your Christian beliefs,' replied Ashmodai. 'As is the rest of me.'

'I don't have any Christian beliefs,' Judith muttered grumpily. 'I'm *Jewish*. And you don't look damned to me, just damned annoying. That was the last of my good coffee.' She had recovered from her shock and she was in prime form. 'And now that you've come, you can go again.'

'Why did you call me, simply to dismiss me an instant later?' Ashmodai looked a trifle surprised.

'I wanted to prove that I could do magic. Without Zoë. And without my bloody son Nick laughing at every step I take. And I *can*.' This last was said defiantly. 'And you seemed a safe enough bet—the note next to that invocation said 'probably harmless'.'

Ashmodai mouthed "probably harmless" as if it was a foul taste, but when he spoke, he addressed the other issue. His demonic manners were marginally better than Judith's human ones.

'You felt that you were incapable of acting without help from your children? You do not do anything alone?'

'I do *everything* alone, thank you very much, even parent–teacher nights. Except for magic, till just now. Magic is too new. And I didn't know for certain if it worked when I did it by myself. There are some weeks you need to strike out and check that life is the way you think it might be. Or might not be.' She looked up at her visitor in vague surprise. The success of her spell had finally communicated itself properly to her brain.

'Such a trivial test is hardly sufficient reason to summon the King of Demons,' his tenor voice menaced. 'I shall haunt you until you discover a dignified reason to have summoned me.'

And he disappeared.

'Hey, I freed you, isn't that enough?' Judith shouted after him.

'Men,' she grumbled as she washed the dishes. 'Never clean up after themselves. Never say thank you. Damn your big toenail!' she flung into the air after the faded royalty.

Judith was too busy with her job and Zoë's musical and Nick's worries about Year 11 to think up idiot reasons, she told herself. Besides, demons weren't worth their weight in ground coffee. He'd gone and that was that. His words were just words, that was all. Not even worth telling the others about, she reassured herself. These excuses worked for a full day and a half.

At the end of that day and a half, she encountered her favourite yellow sticky notes in odd places around the house. 'A reason,' they bled at her sometimes. 'A cause for summoning!' they vampired at others.

The red of a certain tall being's bloody eyes, damn him, was her automatic thought. Not only were the notes written in dripping and near-illegible crimson handwriting, but Zoë and Nick couldn't see them at all. She grumbled to herself each time she found one and had to throw it out. 'Bloody idiot of a King of Demons,' she muttered.

It was one of those times of year, and everything she did was fated to put her into a mood. Her children took one look at her face over dinner and found reasons to go to their rooms. She had only thrown plates at the wall once in their lives, but that once had impressed itself upon them deeply. Nick commented downwards in Zoë's direction as they slunk upstairs, 'I don't know which is worse, when she's like this or when she's being the sweetness and light dream-mother.'

It was a very productive time in the household. Judith in a mood extracted miracle work from tradesmen, screamed at kids throwing stones at cats, plagued the Women's Electoral Lobby, and generally left an impression on the world.

Nick and Zoë just made very, very certain they were not seen in public with her. This meant, of course, that Zoë's homework was done in record time and that Nick rose to a whole new level of brilliance at his computer games. Not something he could boast about to Mum—not when she had been talking carefully at him about which university he wanted to attend—but it let him strut a bit among his friends.

One evening, when Nick was safely upstairs and Zoë was even more safely in bed, the Demon King manifested to Judith.

'If you are not Christian, then what are you?' he demanded, fixing her with his big, brown-red eyes.

'I already told you. I can't help it if your memory is like Swiss cheese,' was her first comment. And then, 'You look like a chronic alcoholic with those eyes,' she accused. She was quite capable of being courteous, but for some reason Ashmodai got right under her skin. 'It's nothing to do with you, but I'm Jewish.'

'And what do you know of demons?' he asked.

'My great-grandmother wrote some notes on demons. Do you want me to find them for you?' Judith said this in a charmingly restrained and helpful voice. To tell the truth, she was somewhat puzzled about what he really wanted.

'That is an unusual way of knowing things,' commented Ashmodai, dryly.

'We lost our family tradition in Dad's garage, and we're reacquiring it bit by bit.' Judith tried very hard to make her voice sound as if she wasn't being defensive. She almost succeeded.

'What does modern Judaism understand about us in general though?' he persisted.

'Why?'

'It is important to me. I have been searching out knowledge of demons in this age and it does not please me at all that the Christian view of us has prevailed.'

'No one's ever really talked to me about demons,' Judith admitted. 'I mean, no one Jewish. Except that Great-Grandma said on the invocation that you were probably harmless.'

'So I do not exist at all in current Jewish thought,' mumbled the demon despondently. Obviously, it was more comforting to him to think this than to dwell on that "probably harmless".

Judith wondered why she would've had a spell to invoke him if he did not exist. He was not an entirely rational being, she pondered, unlike her intensely logical self.

Just thinking of non-existence was having startling effects on his corporeal being. She could see Ashmodai wavering at the edges. Judith felt an odd urge to clap to prove she believed in fairies. She restrained herself and tried a more helpful approach.

'What I know isn't what everyone else Jewish knows, though,' she pointed out. 'I'm Anglo-Australian Jewish, and we have different folk beliefs. Most of mine are in that box on the cupboard.'

'That box? Why do you keep your beliefs in a box?'

'Great-Grandma's notes,' she reminded him. 'We nearly lost them, remember? Now, if you'll kindly let me get to the box, I can tell you what I believe. And then you can make up your mind if you're going to implode, burn the house down, fade away like a Cheshire cat, or behave like a civilised being. I do strongly recommend the last option.'

Ashmodai obediently moved aside. Maybe Judith's personality was getting to him. Or maybe, thought Judith, he really wanted to know. She couldn't see why, though—surely people exist independently of the capacity of others to believe in them?

When he mumbled, 'First encounter in a thousand years and she has to look in a box for me,' Judith began to get annoyed again.

'I'm *Jewish*,' she replied. 'We don't worship false gods or demons in any case. So it doesn't matter if I look in a box, a book or in my own head.'

He smiled at that. 'Some things do not change.'

'Jews not worshipping you?'

'Maybe—I was thinking more of the nature of Jewish women.'

Judith ignored that one. She also ignored the charming smile that accompanied it.

In the box there was a large number of papers. She hauled them out onto the kitchen table, careful to maintain their pristine order. As the demonic hand moved over towards them, she slapped it and said, 'Don't touch. If you want to be useful, make us a pot of tea.'

As she sorted through to find the right page, a cup of tea was placed at her left elbow. It was placed so close to her left elbow, in fact, that it nearly landed straight on the floor.

Without looking up, she said, 'Just behave yourself,' in a long-suffering voice. The voice of the mother of a teenage boy and a near-teenage girl. Ashmodai behaved.

Judith's mind wandered as she skimmed the papers, and she speculated on who had last spoken to the King of Demons as if he were a recalcitrant child. No one since he had been dankly incarcerated, she reminded herself. And before then he had a whole realm to boss. Not that it mattered: she had called the bugger up, she could treat him as a teenager if she wanted to. And if he behaved like one.

At that point she hit the jackpot with the papers.

'Come here,' she instructed the being. 'Look at this page.' It was a list of demons and their qualities.

'Demons are neither good nor bad,' she declared, from the sagacity of three minutes skim reading. 'But most are more likely to not like humans than to enjoy their company—and some possess them when given due cause. If you possess me, you've had it,' she warned banefully. 'I'm a feminist and don't gibber demonically unless I do it all by myself and at my own sincere desire. I am an autonomous being.'

Ashmodai read the list in silence.

Why the silence, Judith wondered? What on earth was he planning? Was he still fixated on the Christian view of his nature? Did that mean that this kitchen was going to be the home of an *Exorcist*-style horror scene? He was reading so very quietly—not a rustle, not a breath. She found him imponderable. Gorgeous, she had to admit, except that he was way too tall.

'Oh!' She was entirely distracted from her wayward thoughts by the next piece of paper she encountered. 'Look, it's you!'

'Me?' Ashmodai, curious to the bone, put the previous sheet upside down in the wrong pile and removed the new one from Judith's hand.

'Someone knows me,' he commented.

Judith snatched the paper back.

'This is *mine*,' she scolded, feeling like an eight-year-old. 'Next time, you can ask. And maybe, just maybe, I'll let you look.'

She read it closely. Ashmodai was mischievous, but not actually bad. He read Torah and was civilised and religious, when he wasn't playing practical jokes. And he was a friend of King Solomon. She didn't know whether to pity Solomon or Ashmodai.

'Why were you imprisoned, then?' she asked, her curiosity aflame.

'None of your business,' he retorted, and they smiled at each other.

'What are you going to do now?' she asked. 'I mean, you're free and I don't want anything from you.'

'It is very undignified for me to be called for no real reason.'

'There was a real reason. I know I can call demons. Without my family. That's reason enough.'

'It is not,' he said inexorably.

Damn it, Judith thought. He's faded again. And left me the bloody dishes. Damn him. And this mess of papers, too. Damn all his toes to nine hells and back.

As she cleaned up and put the papers safely away, she wondered, *What on earth can I ask the demon to do? And what does he really want, in any case?*

She sighed in frustration. He never stayed long enough to say. She bet he was a trickster like Loki and Coyote. Bloody myths and legends. Should never get too close to them. And she would also bet that he was being restrained for him. And again she wondered why. Too much bloody mystery.

Judith kept the pages on demons aside for a while and pondered them. If Ashmodai's dignity was affronted because her reason for summoning was insufficient, she might have to invent a reason to get rid of him.

She put the papers in her handbag and took them to work with her. They weighed on her mind enough, she thought, so she didn't actually have to read them. Judith left them in her handbag the whole day: she was pondering them by osmosis.

Osmosis worked. She realised the key was in the fact that he was a very Jewish demon, and that she herself wanted to know more about things other Jews took for granted. She wanted her kids educated too. She assumed that other Jews took knowledge for granted, anyway. Torah study was essential to Jewish living and all that. And if everyone knew something but her, well, then, it was time to know more.

That night she yelled, 'Hey, Mr Kingie Thingie, I want you.'

'You are not very dignified,' he complained, as he gradually materialised in the middle of the kitchen. On the table.

'Nor are you,' she said, pointedly looking at him. Reluctantly he scrambled off the table. Even more pointedly, Judith wiped the whole table down, slowly and thoroughly.

'Well,' he asked, eventually. 'Have you decided if you want wealth and prosperity or all your enemies to fall? Eternal life or the heartfelt love of a mighty prince?'

'None of the above,' she said. 'And you'd trick me anyway.'

Ashmodai smiled reluctantly.

'I want you to teach us Torah.'

'You do not know Torah?' His voice was slow and surprised.

'I don't even know Hebrew. I told you, my family has some holes in its heritage.'

'I can believe that.' His smile reached right to his eyes, lighting the room. 'So be it,' he said. 'I will teach you Torah. Once a week.'

'Come looking human though—knock at the door and all that. I don't want everyone thinking I summon demons or anything awful.'

Ashmodai laughed and promised. He faded. The table was suddenly covered with sticky notes. *Tuesdays at eight*, they said, the paper blood red and the ink black and dribbling. Very *Rocky Horror*.

Judith damned his right kneecap. She would have to miss her domestic violence taskforce meetings for a bit. This was his revenge for her having found him a task he couldn't fool around with, she bet. Osmosis worked, in its way.

Nick didn't work in his way, however. Nick, in fact, refused to work at all. He was busy trying to hide magic from his new girlfriend, fit in part-time work with full-time school, keep up with his war games, and spend quality time doing nothing with his mates. He wasn't into more complications. Especially not complications that probably required homework.

'Maybe later, Mum,' was his response to the offer of lessons.

'Maybe never,' was Judith's response. She stuck out her tongue at him, as any dignified mother would in a case of minor rebellion.

Kingie Thingie appeared at the door as promised, Tuesday evening at eight. precisely. Dressed in a sharp suit. He was still dark, still handsome, but maybe a foot shorter. Well above six feet, instead of well above seven.

Zoë loved him at first sight. Zoë loved lots of people at first sight. Zoë was, alas, terminally cute. She was soon comfortable enough with her new tutor to snuggle up to him and to gift him with leaves she had found on the street and with her very own flower drawings.

It was in their third class that she asked the inevitable question, 'Where do black Jews come from?'

Ashmodai answered her gravely. 'We can come from many places. Jews come in all shapes and sizes and colours.'

Judith found she could not resist. 'They say even the King of Demons is Jewish.'

The glares they both turned on her were very satisfactory indeed. Successfully annoying both of them at once made the whole demon summoning worthwhile.

Being Other

I am the Other. I am the person you do not see. I am the person you make decisions for. I am the person who receives no confirmation of their abilities or self through normal social interaction. I am lost. I am angry.

I am not what you think. I never was what you think. I chose to be Other. I chose this planet. I chose to be female. I chose how you would see me. I chose my skin colour, my eye type, my waistline. I listened to your words about community and equality. I believed.

I became lost. I became angry.

Now it's time to report home. Soon it will be time to go home. I won't be Other.

I won't be alien. I won't be lost. But I will still be angry. At that moment, I will cease to be invisible.

Don't say I didn't warn you.

Wight Asleep—A Tale from an Alternate Earth

Where had the stories gone? This was the only question Josepha had to answer. The Regent assured her of that, glibly. Just one simple question and he'd let her return to humdrum existence, which he said was preparing to meet society. Her life was so invisible to him. Better than it being a mystery. Mysteries were dangerous.

She'd gone from being someone whose parents knew the royal family too well, to someone who was called on to help the Regent. It was something to do with her being both a magic user and sufficiently invisible, she suspected, since he assumed she wanted her Season in London, to be presented at Court and possibly to wear sprig muslin.

It was almost certainly to do with the long conversation she'd had with him when she was ten, where she'd extolled all the stories in the world and told him with profound sincerity that she could find any of them. The Regent wanted his servants to remain in the shadows. He cast a lot of shade, too. And she'd been an attractive child. Now she regretted that childhood moment of pure theatre.

She still had some of that in her, of course: Josepha determined that when she found the story that he was after she would declaim it from a mountaintop. Or maybe make it happen in real life.

While she determined which would most annoy the man who was soliciting her help, he was trying to explain the problem.

'There are obstacles that I feel you alone will face with equanimity and poise.' He said this sincerely, as if he were talking to his goddaughter. Which she could never be. For this she was profoundly grateful, so she paid close attention to the obstacles he described.

The first obstacle was the year 1648. Not precisely 1648. The Prince Regent was explaining three hundred years of English history in great detail and Josepha shrunk the explanation down to 1648. The essence of 1648 was that the massacres might be something very wrong that was introduced recently, by migrants wearing odd clothes and not speaking sufficient English. 1648 was stories about demons or evil spirits or spells or anything else that entered Britain alongside those who fled torture. 1648 was the first year that anyone had properly documented these incidents.

The second obstacle was so obvious that the Regent left aside the long explanation. In his mind,

Jews in the East were so very different to the Jews of his world that asking one of those who had travelled with the demons and devils would be futile. His subjects were educated, and no one could match them. Josepha tended to agree with this. After all, every single time others had tried to find out what was wrong had failed. Months of misspent effort. That was the heart of this problem. There were rabbis who could be asked, and they were probably wise in their way, but they were not sufficiently English.

There were five people in this meeting besides Josepha, and four of them said nothing. Three of them weren't overdressed and took notes. The fourth was the Merlin, of course. And the fifth did all the talking. To her.

The other people were his people and lived to serve. And to write. She also suspected that two of them had complained that she was female and had been told to be quiet by either the Prince Regent or the Merlin. This was something she could find out, but it was irrelevant.

I'd better do this, Josepha decided.

Britain needed missing stories of strange enchanters. This much was clear. Without the stories, there was no explanation for the evil that had come to England. The wrong explanation had already seen the darkness inhabit the Isle of Wight as if it were its own private garden.

'We've tried Christianity,' said the Regent (speaking for the Council for the Wise, not for the King, which was just as well, considering the state of the King—if he weren't mad, Josepha wondered, would the country be open to such problems?) 'And it failed. If you can return the darkness to night, then we'll reward you. If you give us back the Isle of Wight, we'll give you that arranged marriage you no doubt want, and bring you into Society.'

Josepha would find her own husband and hated all the doings of the Ten Thousand, but her best friend lived her life as if she were a romance heroine and had never been to Almacks. Louisa (the Hon Louisa Peril, of proper Norman heritage… on one side) had a father who had other ambitions and a mother who was the daughter of the middle class. Louisa yearned for an arranged marriage. Josepha thought Louisa was nuts, but if her best friend wanted something… This was when Josepha let everyone know that she didn't just turn up to meetings. Eighteen she was; stupid she was not.

'Tickets to Almacks would be nice for my best friend,' she admitted. 'But I need something else, for me. And are you sure it's the darkness? The darkness doesn't simply put people to sleep.' This was the first time she'd admitted she already knew something about the problem.

She avoided addressing His Majesty's long-term replacement with anything resembling respect. This was what had first drawn his attention, when she was a child. Young and pretty and rude. This took her out of her invisible valley and had led to many things other eighteen-year-old women were unlikely to experience.

As was her wont, she half paid attention while His Royal Highness explained.

'In addition to the Sleepers, there are possessed people in the harbour. Three of them. You can't wake the Sleepers until you can reach them. Deal with the Possessed. Find a way to wake them safely. And no legal cases from anyone's wives and children. Talk to Merlin about your reward,' the Regent said. 'I haven't time. He has carrots and I have the stick. If you don't do this for England, I'll shout to the world that your closest friend is a spinster.'

Josepha blamed her uncle. His gambling evenings were where he'd first displayed her lack of proper behaviour in the Regent's presence. Uncle wore jewels and corsets and airs. Have money, will spend. Have words, will gossip. Not much use for anything else. Being an Old Jewish family had some strange benefits, and she was seeing them all on this very odd Tuesday.

Josepha had until Monday to find her story and, it seemed, to do something useful with it. The fact that Louisa was not the kind of woman who would ever be a spinster was not relevant. The Regent's word carried weight on these matters. Or so the Regent said to Josepha when she objected to the trade.

The Prince Regent pointed out that if the "spinster" tag didn't hold then the "monster" tag would be used. He would bring out all the stories about Louisa's family and make them known. Josepha's choice. 'Or your friend can have her dances at Almack's, be accepted into the ton, and her family reunited.'

Even for the Regent, this was stupid. It was beneath him to make the monster affair part of this discussion. It was an inheritance that was profoundly unnerving to Christian society and it rattled him, she suspected.

Josepha realised that this was the chief reason she had been called in. Christian mages were becoming tarnished when they attempted magic. This Dark was splintering the Regent's world. This meant that her best friend with her underhill (never elven or fairy) grandmother, made royalty nervous. It wasn't the Regent who'd called it "the Dark"—it was Brummell.

Such an elegant name for such an evil happening. Darkness and monsters (that were really elves) had nothing to do with each other, and, Josepha was willing to bet, nothing to do with the Isle of Wight. He needed a solution and was out of options.

What she said was, 'Are you certain it's not the real Dark?'

'I'd never send a young girl into that,' he reassured. His largeness peeked around his corset, giving Josepha equal reassurance. His mother had said how beautiful this man had been in his youth: she couldn't see it. Too Germanic. Too huge.

Josepha left the Regent's presence without even being angry at his leer. Last time he'd done more than leer and ended up with a bruise. Josepha wasn't respectful of royalty. Not even Germanic and huge royalty.

The Hon Frederick Fitzpope, and the current Merlin, who was at least honest, walked Josepha out of the Regent's presence and into her drawing room as quickly as possible. They took tea.

'All I know,' said Fred confidentially, 'is that the three possessed laugh at us when we do an exorcism. Whatever is at play on Wight simply doesn't care about Christianity.'

'Not a typical demonic presence, then,' said Josepha, to her second oldest friend. A generation apart they might be, but they were more comfortable in each other's presence than they should be. Both of them were law-bound by who they were and how they saw the world, and so were frighteningly unable to develop a more intimate relationship. But their friendship was, quite obviously, the reason she was in this spot.

'Nothing from English history. I was thinking about Jewish stories. I couldn't find this… being… in the translated ones, or in any of the English ones but the situation certainly echoes your people.'

'Jewish stories' were the oral traditions from the Continent. There were always more of them out there, no matter how many were written down. There was also the Talmud, but Fred stayed clear of the Talmud and other foreign books.

'My people,' Josepha scoffed. 'I'm English.'

'Oh, God,' said Fred. 'Don't even go there. Think about the obvious. There was that flood of Jews in 1648.'

'They brought stuff with them.' Josepha hated this, and her voice showed it. So did her choice of words—'they' and not 'we'. Her people were those who had never left, even in 1290. Before then some were Norman, and some went as far back as the Roman invaders. 1648 was irritatingly recent. 'So you're saying that there might be more from recent arrivals. Fleeing the Revolution.'

'Not France.' It was Fred's turn to sigh. 'There are other New Jews.' English power came from the natural bond between the Church of England and the Temple. Temple people were acceptable. New Jews didn't see this and so many came to avoid poverty, but also to find entry into one of most the most stable and definitely the largest Jewish communities in the West.

Josepha pointed this out. 'Not my kind.'

'That's why the Regent bloody blackmailed you to do it. He wants one of us to find out what it is and tell us what to do. Or even fix the problem. And it has to be done from within. We can't ask a New Jew rabbi. Too much war. Too much Napoleon. We need that stability to be unshaken. If you fix the problem…'

'It's not a saving souls thing, is it?' Josepha was understandably suspicious of things that required the saving of souls. The missionaries who loved their homeland were far too fond of saving Jewish souls. Even the souls of Old Jews. She'd loved arguing with them when she was a child. Then she found out they were breaking the law in trying to convert English Jews and that, in the fourteenth century and again in the seventeenth century these same soul savers had burned her books. There was no excuse. "The protected people" was a whole canon of English history. Saving souls would be a problem. Was still one.

'Not at all. It's... I can't explain.'

'I'll find you your stories if they exist. Then you can decide what to do with them your own damn self. I'm eighteen.' Josepha wanted a reason to duck out if she needed it, and her age and reluctance would do nicely.

'Language,' said Fred. 'You're a lady, remember.'

'Being Jewish has its advantages. Language is one of them. If I'm going to be borderline, I can swear.'

'If you save England, we'll change that,' he promised.

'How?'

Fred's eyes narrowed, and he watched for her reaction as he asked, 'University degree? In England?'

A degree would give her so many more choices. Most Jews had gone abroad for university. Montpellier, or Italy. But not since the French Revolution or Napoleon. There were two new Jewish colleges for Jewish boys at Daventry and Gresham. Neither Daventry nor Gresham University accepted women. In fact, no university in Britain accepted women.

'We have an agreement,' said Fred. 'Gresham and the Magic Council. To let women study, if you can save Wight. They've already assessed you for Arts Magic and simply need proof of your ability. Saving Wight will give that evidence. You could start next year.'

'And why didn't you offer this earlier?'

Fred grinned, unashamed. 'Because we wanted to get out of this cheaply. Interview with the Regent, a bit of fun for your best friend.'

'Give me all that and the life I've dreamed of and I'll do this. I'll even help you with the Dark, for that's going to take years. You know, despite having talked to the Regent and how much that man annoys me, I don't see how you can even think of it as a reward,' her voice faded into grumble.

'You'll be the first woman ever to graduate from a British university.' Fred's voice only half-mocked. Then he turned quite serious and tired. 'Just get it right.' All the nights he'd stayed up trying to find the stories himself turning his voice from plum to prune. 'This is important. Do it with style.'

'And you've checked the obvious?'

'Everything in English and Latin,' Fred said.

Finding stories in Hebrew and Aramaic was her speciality. Her family had stolen three of the carts of the Talmud, and other books that Louis IX had ordered burned, and smuggled them into England. The family had a certain eminence at that moment, as the royal physicians. They'd been given special allowances and assistance beginning from the 1316 permit. Ten families permitted to honour their religion. Most of them coming from older stock and some coming from very old stock indeed. Those three cartloads were only a fraction of her family library.

She read, and did what she could do without help. Then she sent a note to Fred and he took tea with her. Josepha wore sprig muslin, just to annoy him. He expected her to wear fashionable clothes, and she dressed the way her mother had in 1800 just for him. He refrained from commenting but gave her a speaking look as he sat down.

'It's not one problem,' she explained to the Merlin, as she poured him some tea. 'It's two. The first is some kind of haunting. A traveller brought it in a trunk. The haunting stopped others from getting off boats and seeing what was happening. I've already dealt with that.'

Fred nodded. He had expected no less. 'Tell me what you did,' he said, 'and I'll pass it on.'

'I asked some of my friends if they'd form a minyan and exorcise the three people infested. Our exorcisms need ten adult Jewish men, you see. I was right. Whatever kind of demon it is, it responds to

Jewish exorcism and all three are back where they belong. I've given the trunk to the museum for safekeeping, along with its contents. Now anyone can land, although the three exorcised people are all asleep, just like the rest of the township. From Cowes to Newport, by the way, not the whole island.' Her voice showed just how annoyed she was at having to research this aspect of the problem. 'Anyone could have found that much out by trying to land elsewhere. The only landing place that produces Sleepers is Cowes.'

She refrained from making jokes about cows by sipping her own tea. She also refrained from calling the current government names. Neither of these was at all like her. This was because Josepha wasn't quite finished. The tea gave her a pause to think how to say what the Merlin needed to know without telling him everything. There was another reason for the sprig muslin.

Josepha's ten adult Jewish male friends and relatives had not succeeded at first. The ensorcelled bodies paid no attention to the 'Ahem' from her dignified and polite team of Jewish gentlemen.

'Look at me!' she'd intervened with a shout, mimicking the strongest and most commanding school teacher she'd ever encountered. 'Now you, you and you, pay attention.' Her voice was stern and her gaze steel.

She looked across at the three humans and into their eyes to see the beings lurking. Firmly, she looked. Firmly, each looked back at her, trying to stare her down. One took a step back. The second lowered her head. The third shuddered.

While this happened, her friends began the work. By the time the Possessed had recovered from their encounter with Josepha, the exorcism was almost over.

'I'm not terrifying,' she muttered to herself as she walked off the jetty and onto the Isle. 'Not. Not. Not!'

She and her ten adult Jewish men (who had run such a fine exorcism) had decided to check whether they could help any of the Sleepers, drag them to safety or make them drink. That was when they discovered that the sleep extended such a small distance. Some sort of cocoon protected the Sleepers. Odd, but also a little familiar. Not even those who'd been caught by sleep in the open air were decaying or affected by wind and rain.

Josepha slept on it.

The next day, Josepha sat down before breakfast, surrounded by books, determined to sort this out. She regretted that her hair was down, for its great length and charming curl caught too often. Josepha rang for her maid and ordered chocolate as well as a quick hair styling. Breakfast was irrelevant when there were books to read.

She needed to set up a system. No doubt there would be more evil spirits and other beings appearing now that her homeland was seen as a fine place to live by continental Jews. *Hundreds of years ago we were kin. Now, we're merely connections*, she thought, annotating her current documents with Latin to bring the Hebrew and Aramaic and Yiddish together into some sort of whole. *Speak English and then Ladino, write English and then Latin, pray in Hebrew and Aramaic, know enough Yiddish to recognise an insult.* And ignore the giggling Christian girls who preferred hunting to books. This had been her childhood.

Why were there no girls' schools like Eton? Why weren't girls admitted to university? Why? Why? Josepha felt guilty that she might be the first and that being Jewish gave her advantages. She doubted her friend Jane would ever have this opportunity. Jane was as greedy as Josepha for learning, had a distinct bent for teaching and a need to earn income for her family who lost money when anyone tempted them with a Bubble. But Jane was Christian. Christian women endured so very many more restrictions.

Ben was pulled back into her research by the commentary on the Talmud she was browsing. The solution to the sleeping Wights was in the Talmud, of course. She checked three different versions of the passage and two more commentaries and she was ready.

Her hair being up, she changed out of her morning dress and went to see Fred. With her maid, for this time she was seeing him alone, in the eyes of the world. The other time the absence of people had been due to them leaving the meeting together. And she looked decorous. Proper. Proper manners annoyed her, but had to be done.

The Regent was there, so she had been right to bring her maid.

'Rabbi Choni,' Josepha explained to her select audience, 'slept for seventy years.'

'When?' asked Merlin.

'When Jerusalem was invaded. One of the times. It's not important. What's important is that he slept through all the reconstruction and went back to sleep when he discovered he'd lost everything he knew.'

'I read that last week,' said the Regent. 'Washington Irving wrote it. Rip van Winkle.'

'He took it from us.' Josepha was blunt. 'Irving's not the only one who reads the Jewish stories, so maybe he took it from someone else who took from us. Last time we met for tea Madame d'Arblay told me this happens. She'd never write such a thing, but that's because she says that Fanny Burney is long gone and that it is a sad-hearted and wordless Madame D'Arblay who lives in London. She tells me that I am full of 'sense and sweetness' and that the Jews of England are more excellent than those of France. She tells me about the books others write and it's no concern to her if they destroy my heritage.'

'She doesn't know you very well,' Fred commented. 'How does van Winkle wake up?'

'Choni.' Josepha grumped. 'You mean Rabbi Choni.'

'Well?' prompted the Regent.

'He saw a new carob someone had planted and wished he could see it fully grown. Just before he went to sleep,' said Josepha. 'I think I can make it happen, though it'll take more than a wish. If you want to attend and take credit, come with me to Wight and pay the bill. It will be entertaining.'

Everyone came with her to Wight. The Merlin, the Prince Regent and three dozen people of note. Plus their staff. Josepha herself brought three hundred Jewish adult men with her to Cowes.

They made quite a party, them and their alcohol and their many carriages. Four hundred adults. Mostly male. Mostly drunk. The ferry was merry and the Prince Regent looked happier than he had in ten years. He made the joke Josepha had not made, last time she had visited. The boat he was on was brown, after all, and soon it would be something brown and coming out of Cowes.

When they landed, her adult Jewish men pretended they were sober, and scattered across the sleeping sector of the island in groups of ten. Josepha saw that they were using the maps she had made and was very glad she had made them, and instructions on what to do. She had not expected the Regent's staff to supply so very much alcohol for the whole party, nor had she expected her people to drink so heartily.

First, they each found a sapling, uprooted it with care, and replaced it with a full-grown tree of the same kind. Those trees sobered most of the men up, she saw, as she wandered between several groups.

Each team watered their tree and said a prayer for its health and also the blessing that rejoiced in being safe and well in this season. Then each ran an abbreviated morning service, adding the critical section of the Kol Nidre prayer. This was how Josepha hoped to create the end of a cycle. There were tall trees where there were once new trees, and the annual moment of truth and terror and new beginnings completed the cycle. It was time to start again, all vows and promises null and void.

That should take care of everything, Josepha thought, smugly. *And it sounds good, with those echoes of one of the most ancient and strongest prayers ringing around the island. Make the Regent think it's Big Magic. It'll get me into university.*

'Christian prayers would've worked,' said Fred, as he, too, listened.

'Maybe. Maybe not. The Regent got on my nerves with his 'I've read all the latest writing and it has all the answers.' It had to be Jewish. That way we own our own culture again. Just that scrap of legend.'

'You own the demons, too.'

'I don't mind not owning them. I'll give them to you, if you like. Your New Year's present. Three demons in their own trunk, wrapped in brown paper. If either of us were Christian it could go under a Christmas tree.'

'Things will be quieter when you're at university.'

'Only if they give me enough work. If they don't, I'll come back and help you with the Dark.'

'May the Spirits and Blessings preserve me from eighteen-year-old girls.'

Untitled

This is the way the world ends.
This is the way the world ends.
This is the way the world ends.
This is the way the world…
This is the way…

Damn.
Wiring fault.
Signal not sent. Bombs not dropping. World not ending.

Maybe next time.

Passports

Kristy wanted the ground to swallow her up, but there was no place to hide in that Louisianan diner.

She had been talking to Brigid over pancakes.

'Stop fiddling with your passport,' Brigid had said, 'and focus on me. I know you've been travelling for thirteen weeks and I know you're desperate to get home, but I'm not going to see you for years. Now put that thing away and let's talk.'

'I was just admiring the stamps,' said Kristy, mildly. They were impressive stamps. Six countries in thirteen weeks made the passport look well-used. 'Besides, it's too early for conversation.'

The hour was Brigid's fault. She had convinced Kristy that they ought to start early and to visit yet another plantation.

Kristy thought about her last few days and said, 'I'm sick to death of plantations. If anyone says "the romance of the river road" even one time today, I swear I shall spew.'

The waitress gave her the evil eye. 'It's our history you're talking about,' she said. 'Show some respect.'

Kristy felt entirely intimidated. Despite this, the ground refused to swallow her up. She thought she liked history, but here the past was a bit overwhelming: everyone's anger was on such public display.

She swore to herself that she would not be daunted, even though the two of them were visiting the slave plantation to end all slave plantations; even though she was travelling with one of her closest friends; even though it was her last day and she ought to be committing every second to memory. Deep down, nothing mattered any more. She was historied-out. She was sympathied-out. In fact, all she wanted to do was get out.

Brigid was the enthusiastic one and she was the one who forked out the money at Riveredge Plantation. She went to sort out tickets, leaving Kristy to explore the front of the property.

The water gardens and the buildings and the ornamental roses had to wait until they had the tickets. This left just one place to wander besides the car park. It had the sort of view that movie-makers loved. Had loved. Many times. Bette Davis had stood there on that greenest of green lawns and Vivien Leigh had drowned her ankles in its moistness and probably a thousand politicians wishing to make firm statements on the South had waded through the lush grass.

'The present is so much more important than the past,' Kristy said to herself, defiantly. She thought of the shotgun houses in New Orleans, the ones that would never house anyone again. She thought of whole towns razed by flooding. She thought of poor folks and once-comfortable folks whose lives would never be the same. Brigid had told her about slavery on the drive down. She had discoursed eloquently about Reconstruction and the damn yankees. It was a flood of sorrow.

'Bloody history,' Kristy said, as she looked at one of the greatest houses in the South.

From the slope leading to the river, it looked such a giant mansion. Columns and white paint and covered verandahs. Except she didn't think they would call them verandahs. Some fancy name for some fancy place. Even the little tower-thing at the top was too elegant: it looked terribly eighteenth century. She tried saying it to herself with a plummy Oxford accent, 'Terribly eighteenth century, my dear.'

A guy with glasses turned to her, his eyebrows slightly raised. 'No,' he said, in that raspy voice. 'It's antebellum. Greek revival.'

'Antebellum?'

'Before the war.'

'If ant*e*bellum is before the war then ant*i*bellum would be pacifist, I guess,' Kristy said, brightly. 'Anyhow, that makes it from around the 1890s, or maybe the early twentieth century. 1890s stuff from home looks different, somehow.'

'Obviously you're not from England,' Mr Glasses said.

'No, from Australia. How did you guess?'

'I can't imagine a British person wouldn't know about the Civil War.'

'I stand reproved,' Kristy said, as politely as she could under the dismissive circumstances, and patted her passport pocket for comfort. One more day!

Mr Glasses disassociated from her and moved down the slope to the house, presumably to wait for the forever-delayed tour. She watched him walk through the avenue of oversized trees. She imagined them falling upon him one by one and how he would pick himself up, cartoonlike, each and every time. He would wipe his glasses very clean at the very end, dismissing the oak trees as un-British.

She saw a lady in a hooped skirt walking around past the columns. *Yippee, tour time,* thought Kristy, glumly. As she got closer, she realised that the house wasn't all white—just the columns were white. Everything else was cream and red and charmingly historic. Not Tara, but something friendlier. Kristy rebelled inside herself. Today she didn't want to be friendly with a house. She wanted a quick plane home.

As she got closer, she took a good look at the guide and giggled. What she had taken to be bands of dark trimming at the wrists and an uneven (but very deep) border at the neckline turned out to be a bottle green turtleneck jumper over which the dress had been pulled without due care. The hooped skirt and old-fashioned blouse were trumped by the turtleneck jumper. Riveredge House was the centre of authenticity, it appeared.

The jumper liberated Kristy. It and the vaguely Ivy League accent of the guide. A black guide explaining the sorrow of the people of Riveredge might have stirred her to some respect, but a pale-faced woman who was patently not local explaining what great supporters of the Arts and what gentle people these owners of 1800 souls were, did not inspire such respect at all.

As the Ivy League accent informed Kristy that Riveredge House had sixteen rooms, Kristy's eyes were focussed on the big red wooden gates that hid the gardens. When the introduction to the tour was finished, those gates might even open to let the tour party through. This wasn't her main concern, though: her main concern was to decide if the turtleneck hid a person or an automaton.

It appeared that once upon a time, the view had led straight from the front door to the Mississippi.

The floods of 1927 had intervened. Slaves had drowned and their houses had been swept away, but Riveredge House had come through triumphant.

'There's a local belief,' the man in glasses whispered in her ear, 'that one day the river and its mud will drown the house.'

'So the past is really important to the locals?' Brigid was standing close and couldn't resist the conversation.

'Very important. Denial is dangerous. It leaves people between realities.'

The rest of the group moved inside through a side door and the three followed, slightly lagging.

'So there are many stories of plantation life?'

'Not if you mean slave tales. The stories are more about the veil between the living and the dead.'

'Ghosts.' Brigid was excited.

The man smiled at her. 'It's said that the weight of history is so heavy here that it manifests.'

'Ghosts,' said Kristy, depressed.

'You want to remember they're ghosts,' the man advised. 'It's the people who can't tell the difference between past and present who get trapped between.'

Why did guys assume that sounding mysterious was flirtatious?

Ms Turtleneck called them to attention as she explained one of the parlours.

Kristy paid no attention to the fireguard or the missing piano. Instead, she let her mind romance a little. She thought about the tears of the local Indians and of the slaves. Or maybe of the land enacting its revenge. Or maybe strange local spirits. She couldn't decide what to romance about, really, so she let her mind drift from one topic to another and finally found herself up the dangerous-looking stairs and leaning on the railing of the upper balcony, admiring the oak trees, and was grateful that romancing was all she was doing.

There was an unutterable sadness about all this green. It wasn't as miasmic as New Orleans, but it was too vivid to be real. She patted her passport pocket, then she started reciting Dorothea McKellar. Kristy had just got to 'The wide brown land for me' and was feeling nicely patriotic when Brigid passed her.

'Put a sock in it,' she said. 'Enjoy the place you're in. You'll be home soon enough and you won't have seen anything. You'll have spent the whole time complaining.'

'Disrespecting,' said the tour guide. It seemed very rude of her, but when Kristy looked across she explained, 'I don't mean you. I was talking to the gentleman here.'

It was Mr Glasses. Of course, it was Mr Glasses. *And I bet she does mean me*, thought Kristy. *I can be bloody disrespectful if I want to*, and she thought disrespectful thoughts all the way down the avenue of oak trees before she turned to go inside and admire the map of the plantations of Louisiana.

'Very historical, that map,' said Mr Glasses. 'It has the number of slaves on each property at the time,' and he pointed out the little Arabic numbers, written into the landscape as if they belonged.

In a confidential moment Kristy said, 'I really don't think I understand the slave-owning thing.'

Mr Glasses nodded, surprisingly sympathetically.

Near the map was the dizzying spiral stairway. Kristy was distracted by a young girl who was almost skipping down it. She belonged in this place, and it showed. Her blue dress bobbed and swayed, and she made the old house look almost comfortable.

'Can you tell me where the toilets are?' Kristy called up. The young girl shook her head, and Kristy said, 'Thanks anyway,' and decided to wait till lunch. Food was, after all, only a few minutes away, and the menu had promised salads. Salads were something she was missing, badly.

She found her toilet. A half-hour later she was sitting down to one of those US salads where the greens were hidden so that they wouldn't damage the diner's spirit.

Truly, she was so over travel. This was probably the best of places and she was just not getting it because she was so homesick and so exhausted. What she wanted was to sit in front of a TV set and watch back-to-back episodes of *Neighbours*. Not that she normally watched *Neighbours*, but she would make an exception to feel as if one tiny corner of the vast sphere she inhabited was Australian.

They were about to head into the garden tour when Brigid suddenly realised that she, too, needed a toilet. One always needs toilets at the worst times when one travels. Mr Glasses moved predatorily towards orphaned Kristy and she got caught up in another chat.

'How do you know so much?' she asked. That might keep his approaches from becoming personal. Or it might not.

'My brother was an expert in the folklore of this area.'

'Where does he work?'

'He went missing here, thirteen years ago.'

'I'm so sorry,' Kristy said. It was the first thing she had said with sincerity all day.

'I come here annually.'

And you keep his work alive by telling it to stray females of about the right age. Some people are funny. Kristy really needed a neutral subject.

'Do you know who the little girl is?' Kristy asked. 'The one in the blue dress.'

'I haven't seen her,' said Mr Glasses with precision.

His very caution suggested that he knew who Kristy was talking about, and that there was something he wasn't saying.

Before they all moved off into obedient tourist mode again, he said to her, intently, 'You need to take care.'

'I'm sorry?'

'The weight of history can be heavy here. Remember?'

Kristy had no idea what he was talking about. She had already forgotten what he had said earlier. He was a forgettable person, Mr Glasses.

The rest of the tour was a little odd. *I must be tired. I could have sworn I heard a horse neighing,* Kristy thought.

'Did you just hear a horse?' she turned so abruptly to ask Brigid that she nearly hit her friend with her handbag.

Brigid shook her head, but Mr Glasses commented, 'There was one stabled here once, secretly.'

'Was it a billiard room back then?' Brigid asked.

'Oh, yes. The owner loved racing and wanted a surprise entry to win the local event.'

'Did he win?'

Kristy suddenly saw the questions unfolding forever. *My time is so precious right now*, Kristy thought. *Just stop asking questions*, she wanted to say to Brigid. *Let's get out of here and get me onto my plane.*

'Very much so,' Mr Glasses chuckled. 'The owner made a killing.'

The tour was almost over. No matter how much useful information Mr Glasses poured into her ear, the tour was almost over. Soon she could tick it off on her list of 'things done' and head back to New Orleans for that wonderful plane to Los Angeles which would lead to an even more wonderful plane back to Australia. Home.

She walked down the central hall one last time and waved at the young girl. She was about eight, which was, in Kristy's mind, the perfect age for a child. *One day*, Kristy swore, *I shall have a child just as gorgeous as that.*

Her eyes were still playing tricks, because for a moment she could almost swear that the child was transparent. *When I get home*, she thought, *I shall see an optometrist.* She should get Brigid to remind her, but Brigid wasn't going home for three years: she had a Washington job to go to.

She passed that idiot parlour one last time. She peeked inside and saw that there were three rocking chairs, all swinging in unison back and forth, back and forth, back and forth. *Clever effect.* She turned to point it out to Brigid, but Brigid was already in the next room, getting excited all over again about a chair that doubled as a chamber pot. *Toilet humour,* thought Kristy, disparagingly, when she caught up.

They were let out through a back door and went around the gardens one last time. *Whoever it is who runs this place is determined to give tourists their money's worth. I've seen all this before.*

Underfoot things felt funny. She looked down and saw a dug veggie patch (melons, she suspected, but the plants were not really old enough to tell—she hoped she hadn't destroyed any with her thoughtless trampling). Then she realised that it was just another trick of the eye—she was still on the gravel path, where she belonged. Maybe that guy with glasses was getting to her and she was imagining an ancient vegetable patch? The local Indians, perhaps: Houma? Was that who they were?

'Sometimes, I wonder about my sanity,' she confided to Brigid.

'Huh, I always wonder about your sanity,' her friend said, kindly.

Mr Glasses lured both of them to the front lawn again, to admire the oaks. Kristy discovered all over again that the levee didn't exist when the plantation was at its height. It was constructed with cheap labour during the Great Depression. The trees, Mr Glasses explained, were locally named The Gentlemen, and kept the region stable.

'What do you mean?' asked the voracious Brigid.

'I don't know,' Mr Glasses confessed, cheerfully enough. 'My brother said it. He said that life became much more dangerous after sixteen of The Gentlemen were cut down to make way for the levee. Apparently, there was a belief that they held the dangers of the past away from the living.'

'How could you prove something like that?' Kristy wondered this aloud, then threw a guilty look at Brigid. No matter how hard she tried, she couldn't remain respectful for more than two minutes at a time.

'You can't, of course. We do know that sixteen men died trying to float the trees downstream to sell, and that the day after the felling everyone said that the remaining trees wept like willows.'

There's a pun in 'raising the levee', thought Kristy, refusing to be spooked. The eight remaining trees were very beautiful and not at all gnarled or miserable-looking. Kristy shrugged. Imagination was a funny thing. She took it into her mind to count the trees while Mr Glasses and Brigid talked local beliefs. *I must be tired. Every time I count them they come out different.*

My eyes need time out from all this green, she thought. *And I need a rest. A holiday from my holiday.* Sometimes old jokes were the best.

Mr Glasses moved off again and Brigid moved with him. They talked to one of the other tourists. Kristy stood under one of the trees, feeling increasingly disconnected. *Not in one land or another. I so need to be home.*

Brigid bounced back and whispered, 'The woman over there used to be a local. She says that The Gentlemen care about respect. You'd better watch out. You've been giving cheek to everyone all morning.'

'I've been giving cheek all my life. What would they do to me?'

'Get you,' Brigid said in her monster-voice.

'Oh goodie,' Kristy's voice was drier than a martini. 'I might get to haunt a miasmic green piece of turf.'

'What I don't understand,' said Mr Glasses, unexpectedly close, 'is why everything has to be a joke.'

'Some things aren't jokes,' Kristy said.

'It's the last day of her trip,' said Brigid. 'She flies out of Houston tomorrow. She's homesick.'

Mr Glasses shrugged.

He's fascinated by my mind, Kristy thought, *because it's definitely not my oh-so-hot right ankle. Though I have to admit, that last look he gave was a bit on the worried side. Stupid git. Nice, but stupid.*

She looked back at the house from the safety of the trees. She watched the turtleneck lady and her helper lock up the house. Brigid was heading back to the car.

She thought she saw a shadowy figure in the little window on the right, at the top of the house. They hadn't been shown that section—in fact they had only climbed as high as the big balcony. That figure waved. Maybe at her. Maybe at the sad remnants of the other tourists. Then it pointed across the lawn, to the levee.

She squinted to get a better view of the upper room, but there was no one at all there now. She decided to explore the lawn leading to the levee instead. The lady must have been pointing at something or someone: what was she trying to say? Her feet shifted in the deep grass as Kristy tried to decide what to do. In the end she said to herself, *Three more minutes. I'll check it out. Brigid can wait just three more minutes.*

Then she heard the sound of a horse-drawn carriage, getting closer. *You have a great imagination*, Kristy scolded herself. She ought to get back to the car sooner rather than later, perhaps. They still had to drive through the backblocks of Louisiana and that had been eerie enough on the way here, with all the mangroves and strange little petrol stations and white alien petrochemical globes growing out of the landscape. It would be even worse now she was hearing noises.

A horse neighed, and the carriage-sound cluttered to a halt.

Kristy took a deep breath and looked away from the house, towards where the Mississippi hid behind the levee.

Instead of the levee rising to the sky and masking the horizon, Kristy saw the oaks extended levelly. Beyond them she could see the waterfront. She walked down to the oak alley, away from the house. She was trying to work out what trick of the eye caused the ground to look less like a green hill and why it looked as if there were more trees. She started counting the trees again.

Mr Glasses shouted something from way back. Kristy couldn't hear what he was saying, but she did turn and wave, politely.

'I'm just going to the end of the trees,' she shouted back. 'I want to see the water.'

He started running, but was so slow that he didn't seem to get any closer. Kristy shrugged. She would meet him at the water's edge.

A raven flew down from the first oak. It stopped right in front of her. She eyed it. It eyed her. She was suddenly spooked. She almost turned around and went straight back to the car. She didn't and was rather proud when the raven gave way. *I'm just homesick*, she thought, so she took out her passport and held it safely where she could see it. *What a stupid thing to do*, she told herself, and put it back.

As Kristy walked closer and closer to the water she felt some odd emotions.

First, she felt the weight of time. It trapped her between land and sky. It froze her breath and it froze her body. Everything that she felt was magnified and magnified and magnified again, until her feelings and her pain were the only world she experienced. When they unfroze, she started to walk again, though she no longer controlled the direction in which she walked.

A sharp blade cut into her soul and loosened it. It wedged itself inside her and gradually levered an opening. Soon the small dislocation she had carried with her all day drew her half-frozen body away from the land and the earth and the sky and into another Louisiana.

The only words left to Kristy were, *Empty.... I feel empty.* She fought the emptiness inside and she fought the emptiness outside. She looked for words. She looked for ideas. All she had was a dark blankness inside, one that grew and grew.

She looked up at The Gentlemen. The warm oak foliage sheltered her. In their shelter, she found numbers.

Numbers help fill emptiness, she thought. She counted the trees again, in pairs.

Two. Four. Six. Eight. Ten. At ten the window into her soul opened a little wider. She felt as if there was a void between her and her own past. That something was going to fill that void. She kept walking and counting. There was safety in walking and counting. There was always safety in numbers.

Twelve. Fourteen. Sixteen. Eighteen. A child's voice filled the void. The sound of a horse in a billiard room. The chatter of French and the warm scent of summer melons.

Kristy could not stop walking. She wanted to. She took her passport out of her pocket again, but the action didn't help. Defiantly, she held her passport out in front of her. It might carry her past the between, to safety.

Twenty. Twenty-two. Twenty-four.

She was there. She had reached the water. The trees no longer protected her. Not the live oaks. Not the dead oaks. Her passport slipped from her hand.

Kristy was nowhere. Or she was under the levee. Caught in time. Trapped by the weight of the past.

Then the breath was crushed out of her by the mud and the soil and the weight of the levee. She was caught up in the void. Between. Forever.

Her damp passport lay bedraggled on the rich, green grass at the base of the levee. Of Kristy, nothing else remained.

All My Pasts

Fred,

It seems I have a Situation. I didn't think of it as such until my daughter asked me, 'Daddy, are you and Miss Ransom inheritated?'

Does a ghost inherit a human or does a human inherit a ghost? That's what Adele should have asked. Still, she did pretty well for a five-year-old. She's a good kid, my Adele. She doesn't pay a scrap of attention when the ghost introduces herself as 'Gabe's live-in' to everyone. The ghost is annoying. She likes to go 'woooo' when I'm in the shower. I thought it was the plumbing at first. It wasn't the plumbing. It was my great-great-grandmother amusing herself.

The wife is no help. She thinks it's funny. The wife ought to move out. We've been heading in that direction for long enough, God knows. She confiscated my smokes the other day and gave my beer to the next-door neighbour. My inheritation cheered her on.

The wife will not move out. The ghost will not fade. They like each other. My darling daughter can inheritate both of them until they let me have my beer and smokes back.

This note is to tell you that they can all bugger off (except Adele) and that if you're still coming to dinner next week, say hi to me (in the shed) on the way past. BYO beer.

Gabe

Horrible Historians

Doing a PhD is a pain in the butt. We all find ways of getting through it, somehow.

Everyone else in my department pretty much sticks to themselves. They live in the lap of history and study in the lap of history and love in the lap of history. When they die their tombstones will be inscribed with a pithy phrase from Martial or Virgil, or be calligraphed with an eighteenth-century aphorism. They don't bother with the rest of the university. Some of them don't even bother with the rest of the department; they are immersed in thick description, or methodology, or in the wild, wild ways of historiography.

Stupid gits.

I and my friends are rebels. We have been part of a particularly boisterous 'I hate being a PhD' group since we found each other three years ago. We talk politics, bewail the opposite sex, and never, ever, ever mention the name of our supervisor. Sometimes we drink coffee, but more often than not we drink alcohol. Vast quantities of foul liquor. We are determinedly sane, and our livers are becoming just as determinedly pickled.

Even in our little group, there are distinctions. The scientific types have more money and better wine, and us humanities types have more books.

Some of the science stuff is terribly secret. You can tell who is walking around with a 'classified' sticker on their forehead; they bear an air of despair. This is probably my imagination. It's either create an air of despair, or laugh in the face of the idiocy of high secrecy. And one thing holds true in our little club: one PhD must never laugh at another; we are each other's dignity.

My closest friend in the crowd was Ethel. Poor girl, to be named Ethel. In a gentle and kindly world, she would be doing a solid research project on adjectives in Robert Browning. Not going round with 'Top Secret' marked by the furrows of her brow.

Ethel is our resident Canadian communist mathematician. She says her lack of temperament is because she was brought up in Toronto and the rest of Canada hates her. She tells me, when we get maudlin over coffee, that she is used to being different.

Abstruse mathematics is Ethel's game and she is notorious for playing it as if it means something. Why abstruse mathematics should ever be top secret is beyond me. Why it's studied at all is still beyond me, but I'm polite in public.

One day Ethel rang me. Ethel, by the way, is notable for everything red; she once confided to me that her underwear is red. She takes communism almost as seriously as mathematics. So she must have been wearing red when she rang. I can't see that she would not have been.

She was ringing to announce, in dulcetly mysterious tones, that the ultra-secret experiment which gave her research money was almost ready to go public.

'I am about to be declassified! Isn't it wonderful?'

Silly me, I thought she was announcing a party, and I volunteered those little Vietnamese pastries I always make for such occasions.

'No, not yet. We have some final thingies to get through. And I need you for that. I need your help more than anything. Then you can make those yummy pastries.'

'Why do you need me?' I was understandably suspicious.

'I need you to do our historical sequencing.'

'Huh?' I admit to being surprised. What she seemed to be saying was that the powers that ran her project had conferred and decided that when they went public it would be with style and spectacle. They were planning to run a trial first. And for this they needed me. It appeared she wanted to give my forehead an 'I bear depressing secrets' stamp. 'Why?'

'Because you are the only bloody history PhD I know,' Ethel said.

'Why do you need a history PhD?' I asked.

'Can't tell you why until you say "yes", but it has good pay.'

I nearly said "no". My main claim to fame, after all, is a profound understanding of the audience–narrator relationship in the early Old French epics. Even if somehow the project actually needed an historian, I was only in the history department because my supervisor had moved over from the Modern Languages Department.

'I am a literary historian, you know. I'm not a regular historian.' I said this clearly. This is important in my defence: I said it with vim and vigour and enthusiasm. 'I research medieval literature.'

Whatever I said, it bypassed Ethel's brain. She heard the word 'historian', and that was apparently just what she wanted to hear. Science types do this all the time. No differentiation, and no understanding. Me? Biased? Naturally.

Ethel wanted another woman because, as she explained first over the phone and then over sequential coffees, she works better with women. Ethel would refrain from talking politics or numbers at me, and I would give her raw historical data: a perfect match. There was a significant pay packet involved.

I admit I stopped ranting about other historians and their fetishes when she let drop what the pay would be. Big bucks. Four figures a pay cheque. The trouble with history is one learns very early about splitting infinitives (it's bad etiquette) and one learns even earlier about splitting a twenty-dollar bill (once it's split, it gets spent). Money is always an issue.

Books are just as big an issue. Just before I said 'Yes' to Ethel I found myself lusting after Rychner. I had this mad vision of owning my own copy of his classic study, instead of pawing the library's with intent to steal it away. Yes reader, I committed myself to an unknown project which would probably result in my death and total destruction, and all for the love of Jean Rychner (deceased).

An old-fashioned political historian would have been a better fit, or someone who specialised in the cut of women's garments in 1631. But they got me because of the coffee club and because of Ethel the Red.

Now, my relaxation reading is science fiction, but my real love is Old French epic legends. Gorgeous tales. Named swords. Flawed heroes. Battle scenes oozing with blood and guts. Sometimes they are holy wars; sometimes they are relentless personal vendettas. Always glorious. The stuff of my dreams.

The stuff of my nightmares concerns the "Song of Roland". There are so many big questions regarding it. My greatest at that moment in time was whether William the Bastard listened to the lovely Christianised version we have in the Digby manuscript, or if the tale Taillefer told was closer to the brutal themes of the vendetta epics. In plain English, how close to the written versions was that one, famous live performance?

I am not blathering; I am scene setting. I could do it in decasyllables with a caesura and make it properly epic, but somehow, I don't think you would appreciate that at all. I refuse to write coldly and clinically.

Besides, Ethel says I have to do this. I pointed to the twenty security provisions in my contract and she told me, 'This is not going anywhere. It is for the record.'

If it is for the record, I can say whatever I like then, can't I? Including that at least half the people working on this project are twits. They might know everything about space and time and mathematics, but they are twits.

I did get excited the first time I saw the machine in operation. A big flat screen: history as video night on the set of Dr Who. The first oak I identified in the England on that screen made me realise, with the same utter joy I get every time Roland dies, why I do what I do, and how fabulous it all can be. And then I came down from my high with a jolt as Ethel blithely admitted they did not know where in England it was, or even when. That oak could be in Surrey yesterday, or in Yorkshire five hundred years ago.

'Fine-tuning is this week,' Ethel said, with an unholy enthusiasm. She wanted to give me a technical description of how they managed to haul the past from oblivion onto that screen, but I didn't want to know. I had lost my joy and was suddenly depressed. England has oaks, this very day. Why should I want to know the weird technology behind us not knowing when that oak grew? History for me is about understanding and contact, not about eternity.

'Oaks on the edge of indeterminably fuzzy bushland are not history, they are nature,' I said to Ethel.

'You know what,' Ethel said, with as much anger as Ethel ever has. 'You are a pleb.'

'You know what,' I said, with dignity. 'It is not proper for a communist to call a friend a pleb, and mean it as an insult. I have to admit—reluctantly—that knowing we can see the past is exciting. I just want to know where that damn oak tree is. The theory doesn't mean so much to me.'

'It's a great project, though.'

'It's a great project.' My voice was as enthusiastic as I could make it.

Ethel believed my words and ignored the tone. We went back to my place and celebrated with stir-fry and chardonnay. Ethel cooked, and I drank.

The next day I came into my brand new office to earn my brand new money and was told I had to find a major historical query. Instantly or sooner. Ethel and her various learned superiors were quite specific in wanting a query that promoted the project. It was the icing on the cake; a way of showing off their splendorous work with aplomb. It was, in fact, why I was being paid.

I was informed (on top of the instructions to keep public relations in mind and to avoid controversiality) that I had to come up with a time and place that was sexy. Sexy. The carrot was supposed to be that I would instantly be a world expert and never have to worry about a job. Obviously there are more jobs in the sciences than in the humanities, if simple expertise is sufficient. Anyway, I bit down my comments and I considered my options.

There was only one query that stood out head and shoulders above everything else and that met everyone's requirements. I thought it through: it looked good. Newspapers would like it and it would not rock the religious masses. I put down on my little form (they had designed me a little form, just for the occasion) my carefully considered words: "Song of Roland", 1066 recitation by Taillefer.

When Ethel asked me what it meant, I told her. 'It's just before the Battle of Hastings. William is marching to battle and is bored to tears. His minstrel sings him the most famous epic legend ever. The 'Song of Roland' is hot stuff. Blood and betrayal and agonising deaths in the pass at Roncesvalles.'

William I of England was important enough to meet those warped scientific needs and I knew every word of the first hundred lines of the Oxford version of the 'Song of Roland'. Why else would they ask me for help, if it wasn't to exploit my expert knowledge?

Sorry, that was sarcasm.

And I digress. I always digress. I have never, though, until now, been accused of being unscholarly and slack of mind. Damn these scientists and their misperceived assumptions about what makes an historian tick. Do you know that they thought that history is a simple matter of names and dates and facts and events? God knows how they define literature.

Anyway, they wanted an event and a date, so I gave them one: the march towards Hastings in 1066. They wanted a more famous name to add to that of Taillefer, so I gave them one: William the Bastard aka William I of England aka William the Conqueror. I listed sources they could check for more information about the subject. I even gave them the precise thing we were seeking with this particular query: what version of the "Song of Roland" William was enjoying en route and how it was performed.

I wrote two paragraphs on the scholarly importance of understanding the difference between oral tradition and written text and then another two on the possibility of an historical narrative about an event and what happened in the event itself being different. I discussed the possibility of "Roland" being sung as opposed to "Roland" being recited or chanted. I listed as a secondary objective the need to find out if Taillefer had William as his sole audience. I listed dialect and pronunciation as aspects to note—was he listening in Norman French or the French of France?

Someone annotated my form—'Why not English?'

I got the annotated form back and stared at it. I did not like being the victim of someone's ill-conceived hilarity. I added a rude answer and returned the form.

We had a meeting at that point. A rather angry meeting.

It appeared that the Middle Ages were perfect, and William was a joy and a delight to the soul of all thinking time-machine operatives. William the Conqueror and the Battle of Hastings and the "Song of Roland" were names to conjure journalists. But they wanted to hear something in English. That comment on the form had not been someone's attempt at wit.

'Modern English wasn't around then,' I explained, in the simplest Modern English I could summon up through my red haze. 'Even if it had been, William would not have spoken it because he was Norman. I can find you another medieval query,' I offered. 'But you will still need a language specialist to interpret anything prior to the Great Vowel Shift, whether it is an English event or not.'

I was very proud of my plain English.

Ethel's supervisor asked for a translator. Ethel—very hot and bothered—asked what the Great Vowel Shift was and why it was so important. I was on my best behaviour: I gave Ethel my biggest smile. I just adore the Great Vowel Shift for English and the Second Palatalisation for French. I talked enthusiastically about language change until the natives got restless.

Ethel said quietly, 'I'm not quite sure we're getting the finer points here. I see that you're saying that there is a potential language problem. You're saying that our ancestors spoke ancestral English, not Modern English.'

I gave her my happiest grin.

Bliss, however, was transient, because someone instantly said, 'This Hastings thing is perfect, you know. I don't think language is an issue.'

I don't know if it is my tendency to temperament, or the fact that I am very unimportant in the absolutely scientific scheme of things. Every scientist in the room was so certain I was wrong. Except maybe Ethel.

I lost my temper.

I had given them an outline of the languages of the time and place, and I had given examples of the various languages. I had even shared the Great Vowel Shift with them. Surely they could see a thousand years ago, after all—what was the problem? I caught a glimpse of myself in a window and my face was as red as Ethel's socks.

I couldn't say a thing, though. All those scientists were so positive that the conversation was over and that they were right. I was silenced.

Poor Ethel was set to doing all sorts of early location of event. I was sent back to work on my thesis, because the budget did not run to having me on the project more than four hours a week, and besides, I irritated the Powers-that-Weren't.

Then the project leader called me in for an interview. An event had been decided on for the launch. The Battle of Hastings looked like a goer. The science was perfect.

He kindly informed me, 'Right now, we are ready to rock and roll. Your job is finished. We are keeping you on the books so that I can get you an invitation to the launch. You are part of the team, after all. The Prime Minister will be there—maybe I can introduce you.'

Everything was just dandy. He was up himself and on a roll; me looking across at him with gloom and doom in my gaze didn't change his view. It did get me called an intellectual snob.

The thought was *Army with famous leader listening to famous story = Launch.* Mr Great Scientist even joked about how the newspapers would probably include a few words of the tale that William was listening to. *Only if they know Old French*, was my thought.

But I had made my point and the point had been ignored, then I had been insulted, and now I was stuck listening to another stupid prosing git. Time to speak out.

'You may very well have an event, but you aren't even near an answer to my original question yet. You won't get a single historical study from that launch, however many hands the Prime Minister shakes.'

'Why?'

'Insufficient data,' said I, trying to sound scientific, then I blew it all by adding, 'I can't see anything in that bloody screen except oaks.'

I got a 'Trust us—we are scientists. We will have that answer for you very soon.'

And pigs might fly. He wasn't listening. I gave up. I went back to my thesis and made as much progress as I could, while I could. Because if they didn't call on me before this launch, then I was not as bright as I thought I was. If the launch were not postponed somewhat, I would also have been surprised.

I was not surprised.

Ethel soon found out what my saying I was a literary historian meant in terms of looking at the cute flat screen of a past event unrolling. It meant I filtered all my medieval knowledge through literature. Mostly poetic. Ethel showed me a meandering army moving slowly across the screen, and asked me to tell her all about it.

'There are men on the screen,' I said. 'I can tell you how epic heroes declared battle,' I volunteered after a bit of thought. I wanted to be helpful. Truly.

'Look at the screen,' Ethel pushed. 'Tell me what you see.'

'I see men. And they are marching. Well, maybe not marching. Maybe just sort of walking and riding and stuff.'

That was when she threw a pen at me.

I fell into a sulk. I went straight to the library and found her a reproduction of the Bayeux Tapestry, but I did not invite her to my place for dinner. I went back to my little office and buried my head in my new copy of Rychner and I cried.

Soon she reported back to me that William was not wearing the precise gear depicted on the tapestry on the exact day of the army marching through Ethel's big screen viewer. Surprise, surprise. I gave her some reasons why this might be so. I think she listened. Maybe. I didn't care.

Ethel said, 'You know what is wrong with this picture?'

'How the hell should I know,' I grumbled. 'It is a perfect bloody picture.'

'I guess I was not expecting so many men in disarray. Or so many horses.'

'How could you not expect men and horses?' was my immediate answer. 'We are talking an eleventh-century army, and one where the very disembarking of the zillions of horses from squillions of boats is famous. The whole economy was bloody horse dependent.'

'Well then, the horses ought to be bigger.'

I did a bit of research (knowing nothing about the size of horses in the eleventh century) and ordered her a copy of Ann Hyland's book. She was on her own from there. Well, with horses, anyhow.

I was very angry with everyone. I can read languages long dead and I can decipher strange scripts. I can interpret poetry and understand the role literature plays in society. None of this had prepared me for that humiliating moment when Ethel wanted me to interpret a straggling army.

From the moment I had buried my head in Rychner until the time when I banged at my computer to order her the Hyland, I had suffered nightmares of gentle hills and pleasant streams and men in clothes that I could have identified if only I had been a different type of specialist. Men marching, men riding, men talking, men walking, men picnicking. I couldn't even call them "stupid gits" with any enthusiasm.

I was not the only one in trouble. My thesis progressed faster than the project at this point. Ethel missed all her party meetings for months. Her red was fading into flushed scientific pink. She even missed our rebel PhD meetings.

The launch was postponed twice and finally put on hold. A vague picture of men and horses and lots of baggage tramping on a wet day in England was not quite what was needed. Finding the right army had only been the beginning, it appeared. They wanted a crucial moment, not a lot of mud.

This is when I finally worked out that scientists lived in a science fictional reality. Real history has mud, not moments.

Every couple of days I would get a phone call or an email from Ethel with stupid silly queries. I call them stupid and silly because it was patently obvious I couldn't answer them. Some of them I could help with, and then Ethel would extort more money to pay for the time. I would research for a bit and answer most of the questions and then I would pretend that the whole project never existed.

It was at about this stage that I realised that in Ethel's science fictional world, experts in other fields know everything about everything. They were plot devices used to advance proceedings, and not proper specialists at all. I had to tell her. I walked into her office, without knocking. I looked down at her, at her desk, and she was a bit wan.

I said, 'You are coming for coffee.'

'Why?' She was almost curious.

'I have had an inspirational illumination,' I declared.

She smiled a trifle at that, and came for coffee. Over this sobering drink I informed her about my new deep thoughts.

'I am not a plot device,' I announced. 'If you want real help, you might want to try asking me questions about things I am likely to know the answers for. If you keep asking me things outside my specialisation, then don't blame me if dramatic scenes of major historical import fail to show up on your device.'

There was a dull silence. This was not going down well. Maybe I should have bought her some chips to go with that coffee.

I suggested, 'If your budget doesn't extend to asking experts on each and every subject your project people have questions about, then maybe it could run to mind-expanding drugs at your end, because that way you will at least get emotionally satisfying answers.'

It was a nicely-phrased sentence, I thought. It did, however, lead to Ethel sulking, as night follows day. Her face turned pink and clashed with her clothes and she got up from the table and walked away. Back to her office, I assumed. We were not on speaking terms until the project forced her to contact me again, at which point we made up.

I have no idea how Ethel finally sorted out the order of march and how to identify Duke William, or anything, to be honest. I did what I could when I was asked, but I think the reality of that research was cold hard slog at Ethel's end. Anyway, she did it. It took her six months, but she did it. Eventually she found William being sung to by Taillefer, *mirabile dictu.* Located it in her space-time mathematics and allocated it whatever she had to allocate it to find it again and that was that. We were finally ready to rock and roll.

This is when the powers that be realised that I am not a liar: they could not understand a word that was said to William of Normandy by anyone in his vicinity. I couldn't help. What with everything being so long drawn out, I had only six months to submit my thesis.

They had secrecy provisions and refused to get in anyone else. I—and no one else—was their "Technical advisor (historical sequencing)". They twisted my arm. I cursed all scientists to one of the more dire hells. 'The Deluge will target scientists next time,' I informed them.

They tried to bribe me. I pointed out that they had pointed out that I would not be employed by them afterwards. I said I needed to finish my doctorate if I wanted to get a job someday.

I submitted it a week ago. Thank God it is over, is all I can say.

News about me submitting must have got through the system, because yesterday I was offered two months' work. Lots of nice pay.

My first task was to write this up. My next task is to watch the scene however often it takes to write a guide to it, so that, when the launch finally happens, the scientists have a cheat sheet. They are going to pretend they know it all, including Old French.

Before the first task came the viewing. Ethel and I and Ethel's boss watched William listening to Taillefer.

I am going to write down what happened, because it is not my fault and I refuse to take blame for it.

I was in the TV room, waiting for the big screen to flicker. I had a notebook in my hands and my dictionary on my lap. They showed me the scene.

In that instant, I was the first living person who knew Old French to actually hear it spoken. I didn't understand everything, and what I thought I understood definitely needed checking. There was something very wrong.

'Can I see the scene again?' I asked.

When I got a huffed "What for?" as a reply, I explained that, 'We only know Old French as a written language, and I need to accustom my ear to it to be able to translate. I need to see the scene several times more, at least.' There was no way I was going to write that report without being certain.

The techies were not happy with me.

'It takes lots of programming to get an image—we can't just rewind it like a video,' they told me.

'You couldn't just point a *video camera* at the screen?' I asked.

This got some embarrassed mumbling; turns out they had the video equipment, they just hadn't set it up yet.

They were saving it for the launch. *Stupid gits.* I pressed on. 'I am the first person to make out even a single one of these words since they were said,' I said. 'I can write you down some phrases, but there is no way I can understand exactly what is being said in one hearing.' I thought I did pretty well to pick out some words and phrases and the general gist of things, but no, the techies wanted more. They wanted everything, instantly, in one viewing. I was not happy.

I put my notebook on the floor and stood up.

'I can't give more,' I said. 'I need that scene again.'

I kept on saying this until they understood it. Except that they refused to accept it even when they understood it. We all stood there arguing and waving our arms.

Then Ethel's supervisor joined in. He is a big bloke and moved closer and closer to me as he made his point about the technical issues.

'We can't rewind things like a video,' he said. 'It takes hours to recalculate and reconfigure, because each and every time we look, we are starting from a new point in *our* time.'

It was all very logical. Except that he kept moving towards me as he was speaking, and he loomed over me and poked at my shoulder with his finger. I was entirely intimidated. I stepped back, and back, and back. I travelled right across the room in the space of three sentences.

Then I resolved to hold my ground. I couldn't do any more than I was doing, intellectually, but I could stop backing away. So I did. He responded by coming close again and poking his finger harder than before.

'You can see the problem,' he said, poking at me. 'It takes resources to recalibrate.' Poke. 'It is difficult.' Poke.

I took one last step back, towards Ethel.

I fell onto Ethel. Ethel overbalanced.

Guess where she fell.

I found my balance just in time to see the big flat screen shoot sparks and die. The first thirteen-million-dollar argument of my life.

It is a great pity they have a spare screen. Lots of machinery money, no money for historians. Bloody scientists.

At least, however, I will be finished with them in two months. Leaving the spare screen behind ought to distress me unutterably because, really, it is very exciting to look at the past on the time machine. But it doesn't distress me at all. I don't want to know. I have to record everything, so I am going to record this, but I am rather pleased I signed those twenty security clauses and can't go public.

You see, there was a real problem with my first viewing. I strongly suspect that William was not sung the heroic and glamorous 'Song of Roland' on the way to his great victory. I identified several words very clearly during that first viewing.

They all described genitalia.

Lucy's Adventures on the Fourth Colony

Twenty years of terraforming. Twenty years of hazard reduction. Twenty years of research and testing. After sixty years, the bureaucracy deemed Digon ready for settlement. It was the fourth colony.

'I don't want to go.' Lucy was adamant.

'You don't have a choice,' said the mistake she had married.

Jason wanted to settle the stars. Jason was not averse to emotional blackmail. He had always dreamed of living on Digon. Always. He stated this. Then he stated it again. He did not stop stating it until Lucy capitulated. Reluctantly.

This is how Lucy found herself in a cardboard cut-out building, near a cardboard cut-out spaceport, cosseted by a cardboard cut-out culture imported by the technical teams who had settled first. *Scientists have no idea of civilisation*, Lucy thought, as she travelled from the cardboard spaceport to her cardboard house.

When she stepped out of her cardboard house that first morning, she took a deep breath. It caught in the back of her mouth. Her throat felt big and blocked, as if she had cried for hours.

'You're emotional,' Jason said.

'I'm not sure,' said Lucy. 'It hurts to breathe.'

'Don't be stupid,' said Jason. 'You're just trying to spoil it for me. This is my dream come true.'

'No,' said Lucy. 'It hurts to breathe.'

'Stay indoors, then,' said Jason, and went to his new workplace leaving Lucy alone and breathless.

She experimented. Indoors was fine. Outdoors hurt.

Lucy nodded. 'That must be it. I might stay indoors for a bit. Get used to the idea of Digon.'

'This is ours,' said Jason, proudly, about their runabout, which was all chrome and curves.

Lucy smiled at him. She let him show her all its gadgetry.

'You know,' Jason said, abruptly, 'about what you said before. Nest if you must. You don't even have to go outside to get into the runabout— it has an airlock and filters.'

'There's something wrong with Digon air?'

'Not a thing. Digon's terraforming was thorough. This baby was made for Salya. The airlock makes you feel secure, that's all.'

Nesting sounded nice. She dwelled on the thought, of the safety in the sheltering curves of the runabout.

Not a mouthful of Digon air entered Lucy's lungs. At first it was because it hurt to breathe when she went outdoors. After a few days, it was because Jason wouldn't stop to talk and because outside hurt her artist's eyes. When Jason carelessly left the little runabout behind when he went about his important colonial business, she did the shopping. At all other times, she stayed indoors. After three months, Lucy felt as flimsy as sun-bleached paper.

Jason focussed tightly on his new project. Lucy agreed she'd manage the house. Once a fortnight a freighter arrived with a trunk of their possessions. Each trunk became an excuse to put off starting life on Digon. On their first wedding anniversary, Lucy looked at her husband as if they'd been married a lifetime and realised that he was wholly immersed in Digon and its development. He was not immersed in Lucy.

Until Jason understood this, until Jason stopped and listened, she couldn't go outdoors. So Lucy kept trying to adjust, from indoors. She could have replaced the swims in the ocean and brisk winter walks in the park that she missed from home with the ocean on Digon and the parks near her new home, but the whole of Digon was a colourscape on canvas.

Every day she was that drab dark paper. Every day she was less Lucy.

Lucy needed a divorce, but divorce would not get her to Earth. And she could not support herself on Digon. Digon's economy was carefully designed to give its inhabitants houses and runabouts, not savings and long space journeys. It was also not designed to give jobs to its colonists' spouses. The couple clung together by sheer force of will.

Lucy was cool to the Jason-clones who insisted on visiting. Warm brown eyes and cold souls, every one. Not real. They acted as if she were the only woman in the whole colony. 'Puterhead Lucy, who spent all her time designing imaginary worlds for glossy old-fashioned books. 'Puterheads were not the stuff of men's fantasies: she knew that and paid no attention to them.

Lucy clung to Jason because she saw herself fading to drab.

Jason clung to Lucy because he was suspicious. He refused to listen, but he didn't refuse to talk. Every time he met one of the Jason-clones, his tongue bit and tore and ripped her to shreds. Three times a week she cried herself to sleep. Lucy was bitterly and boringly loyal, and Jason should have realised it when she had given up Earth for him and for Digon.

'Pity about the loyalty thing,' Lucy reflected, as she prepared dinner. Pity left a trail of blood in the kitchen as Lucy sliced into her fingers by mistake. She let the water run and run and run over her fingers until the water was clean. Her fingers dried into desiccated parchment. They were fading and bleaching and eventually they would disintegrate. Such was wedded bliss.

The last trunk from Earth arrived. It contained fragments from their courtship and the honeymoon. Little hearts on a chain from Jason to Lucy. A small card of exquisite design from Lucy to Jason.

Jason's proposal lay underneath the small card. She picked it up. Jason had left a red paper doll and a note on the hotel bed when they were in Japan. Lucy didn't need to unfold the note. "This is a wedding doll," it said. She knew it by heart. "Marry me."

Her tears fell onto the doll. A drop of the red dye fell from the doll onto the folded proposal.

That evening, Jason's voice was tender. He had a new project that sparked him with life. She couldn't break his happiness; she couldn't tell him what was wrong.

"Lucy still loves Jason," she wrote, then hid the paper behind the marriage proposal.

Lucy still loves Jason. She loved the way his eyes brightened when he talked about developing new strains of wheat. She loved the pure grace that was the shape of his jaw. Lucy created a small shrine to their marriage, using the doll and trinkets from their courting.

One day Jason held the tiny doll and asked it questions with his eyes. Lucy smiled.

'What is it?' Lucy prompted.

'Earth,' Jason said. 'These are all from Earth. We're on Digon now.' He dismantled her shrine.

Lucy moved to the couch: bed was too unhappy. She wanted to ask someone if this was proof of a failed marriage, or if there was worse to come. She wasn't sure she could handle worse.

There was no one to ask. The only women Jason introduced her to were scientists twenty years too old for stupid questions.

Lucy did her best to find a different solution. She sent design after design for product after product into the space between the stars. She drew unicorns and griffins and strange dream-creatures. Somehow, her agent found her pictures and slowly transformed them into money. Not enough money to leave the planet. It would never be enough to leave the planet.

That was another thing Jason had neglected to tell her. A good income on Earth, on Digon was just enough for the small luxuries that kept her soul from being pressed into confetti. And Jason, as company man and scientist, didn't notice because he had what he needed. He had his work and his time playing corporate games in luxury hideaways.

Why does a colony have luxury hideaways, Lucy thought, *When I can't buy decent art supplies?*

Finally, finally, finally, one of the science women peeked into Lucy's hiding place and said, 'Come to a party. Tonight.'

Lucy went and was surprised to find that she enjoyed herself. She walked in the night. She tentatively breathed real air. Digon might become comfortable in time. Might be possible. All things were possible. This was the puffed-up valour of being the only young woman in a crowded room and being crooned over and cared for. Puffery made even Jason possible.

The next day she took the little capsule runabout and shopped. Cardboard cut-out shops. Oddly reassuring.

Could be home, Lucy thought. *Almost.*

Lucy had to carry her parcels indoors. The little space from her runabout to the front door seemed suddenly big. Digon air. Depressing. Then Lucy thought, with a lift, *I breathed Digon air last night for ten whole minutes*. She emptied her little runabout in a flash, loading herself with parcels.

The sun came out. The slight breeze blew warm. It was faintly scented with the pollens and spores of spring. Lucy took a deep breath.

The next breath was shallower, and the one after that hurt and made her rattle. Lucy found enough strength to open the door and crept inside. She sat on the floor and feebly kicked the door shut. Her parcels were everywhere, splattered and piled and scattered. Lucy didn't care. She spent the next half hour propped up by the wall, trying to get filtered air into her paper lungs.

When her expanding lungs returned a measure of intellect to her brain, she rang the doctor.

'Some sort of lung problem,' he said. 'Maybe asthma.'

'I've never had asthma,' said Lucy.

'Maybe it's common on Digon.'

'Maybe?'

'I arrived here last week.'

He didn't have any answers a few weeks later, when Lucy again went shopping in the sunshine and the air faded from her lungs. He called for tests.

The results all came up negative. Except oestrogen. She had too little oestrogen. Then her period came and she had too little oestrogen no longer.

Lucy tested wonderfully negative to everything they had tests for. And they had tests for everything except for Digon itself. Digon was the jewel of settlement because Digon was tested for sixty years before settlement. Digon was the safe star settlement. The advertising said so.

The doctor wondered aloud if it was just stress. 'Young women, you know,' he said, in an avuncular way, 'are prone to being overemotional. Perhaps it's hormonal.' Since her period had just begun, Lucy didn't argue. She couldn't argue. The fates were against her.

Jason was not happy that his healthy wife needed care. It upset the sad equilibrium. 'Come on, you're imagining it. Get a grip on reality.'

Lucy didn't argue. There is no arguing with a doctor who believes that women will joyfully pre-menstruate themselves to an early grave or a husband who won't listen. She would have to find out what was wrong herself. And until she found out, she was damned if she would leave the house. Jason could sulk himself into the record books because he had to buy groceries, but she would not even use the runabout.

Jason was a man who did not believe that wives could fall ill. Lucy wished she'd realised that before they married. She wished there was a way off Digon.

In the meantime, she had to research. The moment when air ran out had been terrifying and she was angry with herself for being scared. Reasons needed discovering.

Lucy found nothing useful in the plant studies and in the general environmental studies for Digon. Also, databases might be her new lovers, but God, they were boring. She designed a nifty little program for turning her data into pictures. She wondered what the Digon population would look like as a monster.

It was a very warped database. It made a very warped monster. Purple for women, of course, and green for men. So many more men than women. The ratio was twelve to one, the same as the Acadian population in the reign of Louis XIV. Typical bloody colony.

Except the monster had the shortest and stumpiest legs Lucy had ever seen. Which part of her data set made up the legs? Children. This was odd.

Lucy dug further. The few children on Digon were all apparently conceived soon after the mother's arrival. The romance of a new planet at work. And Jason had missed the boat. No sex: no children. Lucy laughed.

Then Lucy looked at her data more closely and her laughter died. Ratios of women arriving to ratios of men arriving were about equal. So why was her monster warped? Why was there less purple in its makeup than green? Nothing added up. Nothing.

The lack of purple was deaths. Fatalities hidden beneath other data so that no one would notice. Deaths. Thousands of mortalities. More women under age fifty-five had died than any other group. Deaths. No cause was known.

Lucy was scared. The “unknown cause” list was mostly women of childbearing age. Her age. Her mouth felt dry and she took a deep breath to prove there was air. She made an appointment with the Governor, then called back.

‘I can’t leave the house. I’m not well,’ she explained.

‘The Governor will come to you,’ Lucy was told. Had they been tapping her data use? Or had the doctor blabbed? No matter. Lucy tidied the house and made ready for answers.

Lucy was charmed by white hair and blue eyes. Elderly women were easy to talk to. Until they started saying, ‘Yes, dear. We think that women might have to stay indoors until they cease to be of childbearing age. One of the small quirks of settlement.’

Small quirks? Lucy found herself asking the unaskable, ‘Compulsory restraint?’

Apparently “where necessary”, and apparently they were hopeful of an answer to “the problem” in maybe twenty years. 'We don't have many resources to spare, you see, since we're such a new colony. If we can't find an answer, we'll eventually configure new towns so that women can lead full lives indoors. Until then, we'll make do.'

"Not our fault" was annoying. But "we are doing all that can be done" was demeaning. Even half of "all that can be done" would have left her on Earth, her marriage failed in the very early days rather than in the latter part of the early days. And she would have been able to walk in the sunshine and breathe it in without her body crumpling like paper.

And not telling new colonists, letting them walk in the air as if it were safe: that was criminal.

Stubbornness rose in her like a battle cry. Lucy wanted the choice to walk along the streets. Then self-preservation crept in and her brain caught up with her ire: her oestrogen had been low.

Lucy asked the Governor, 'Did the original scientists allow for hormonal changes?'

'Surely. There were women in the scientific teams.'

'Were they typical though?' A blank look. 'Were they on some sort of medication? Progesterone?' More blank. 'Did they menstruate normally, dammit?' Lucy took a moment to compose herself. The Governor was not paying attention and her face showed it.

'Could there be some allergen that interacts with a specific level of oestrogen?'

'Get back to you on that,' was the terse reply.

Lucy had to wait two claustrophobic weeks. When she received her answer, she stared at the words, her mouth compressed into a thin line. Lucy had been right. Lucy did not want to be right.

The first menstruating woman on Digon had been a colonist. She had died two weeks after landing.

Lucy could see how Jason had missed seeing that his wife was at risk. She could see it in so many places, now she knew to look.

The reasons for preventing normal menstruation had been outstandingly good. Mostly to do with stable physical environments for reliable tests and the ethicality of allowing pregnancy before full colonisation. Terribly rational. Terribly stupid.

When it came down to it, though, those reasons were excuses. She had been the focus of Jason's life and now Digon was. The truth was that Jason was Digon and Lucy was Earth.

Lucy divorced. She paid for the long voyage home using the money she was given for her silence.

Some Thoughts

It's very strange seeing my life laid out on pages. It doesn't look like my life. It looks like print on paper, or pixels on a screen.

When I was eight, I knew I wanted to be a writer. I've told this story so often it feels fictional. How I walked past my grade 2 and grade 3 classrooms (for I was about to go to the Big School) and how I said to myself, 'I can't make a living as a writer. I need to write part time.'

I spent the next years trying to find out how I wanted to earn money. It had to include history, but apart from that, I didn't know. I dreamed of palaeontology and of museums. I still dream of palaeontology and museums.

I like to think that I've not grown older since then, but this collection proves otherwise. The child who wanted to be a writer when she was eight had a strong personality, and that's been a consistent nuisance to me. But the path has been a lot more interesting than my early life suggested. I usually describe my life as a rollercoaster.

I won't talk about my life or my novels or my nonfiction here, except where they run alongside my short fiction. You'll mostly meet them in the Big Gap. Some people have a gap year: I had a gap do-not-ask-how-long in my writing history. In that gap I did some fascinating things, but publishing was not one of them. This is why there is a whole bunch of stories that are being published here for the first time alongside those that were published in the year they were written. Some of them were accepted for publication too many years ago to put a number to, and are still being published for the first time. My stories hide so many stories.

I've just scrolled through the draft file for the first time and, until then, I was going to give you a deeply passionate argument to explain everything, because that's the way I analyse my novels when occasion demands. Several thousand words profoundly connected that say… something. Occasionally meaningful. Always verbose. That's my more academic self.

Looking at this collection, I find it's hard to describe my work that way. Someone else might be able to be passionate and lengthy and deeply intellectual about my short stories, but it appears that I think about my short stories, and the part of my life they encompass, as vignettes.

Vignettes. You're stuck with vignettes. I'd apologise, except that you could use this as an excuse for coffee. A new cup whenever the story changes. I'll apologise for over-caffeination then, not for the vignettes themselves.

My first story was not a story, but its appearance was.

Let's start at the very beginning. "Summer Job" was my first publication that wasn't a letter in a newspaper. I didn't mean to write it. It was originally printed unchanged, in *Kivun*. Reading the published version, I discovered my passion for editing. I played with the story over two years, and one of the variants is included here. All my stories have stories, but the origin of this one is sweet. Sometimes the world is a good and caring place and lives can change.

I gave up on the thought of writing when I was a teen because I was told I was no good. I wrote poems and they went into the school magazine and I got top marks in English, but an aunt who was a much-loved senior English teacher discouraged me, and the family trusted her judgement. When I was fifteen, therefore, I stopped writing for anyone else because, in my small world, there was no reason to publish. I wrote travel diaries and private journals, for I cannot actually stop writing with any degree of comfort, but I gave up on my plans of being a writer and I worked extra hard at school and I was totally miserable.

At the end of first-year university, there was a summer camp for Jewish students. There were arts and crafts and a lot of discussion of all kinds of things. If anyone ran such a camp today, I'd say, 'Let me teach', because it changed my life. I've written about my encounter with Chaim Potok elsewhere. The Potok story is more interesting, but Serge Liberman is who you're getting here. Both of them gave me back my writing.

I'd finished my weaving workshop far too early for comfort (it was bad weaving, but all I had wanted was to get my hands on that loom and so I didn't really care) and was half-thinking of a second piece. My friend Mandy said, 'They're starting up a writing workshop and I so want to go. Please keep me company. I don't know anyone.'

The writing hut was hot. Every hut was hot. It was one of those weeks where cool is fictional. I looked at the assembled group and thought, *This is far too many people for this room.* Serge Liberman was the teacher and he obviously thought so too. He looked around at us and said, 'For the first forty-five minutes you can go wherever you want and write anything you like, as long as it's about clowns or a factory.'

I'd spent the earlier part of summer in a rubber glove factory, so I chose the latter, and scribbled for my allocated time. We all came back and we all read our pieces. There was applause. There were comments. My reading caused a void of sound and movement. I thought, 'Was it really that bad?'

The friends I asked said, 'No. But we didn't know how to react to it.'

As we left our workshop and went to do other things (my next bit of learning was Felix Werder teaching two of us Mahler—this was probably the most privileged week of my life), I was collared by the bloke who'd sat in the back of the room and said nothing. 'I'm Leon Bach,' he said. 'I edit *Kivun*. Type up your piece and we'll publish it.'

Serge found me during the evening and we walked for a while. He explained that he had no idea if I could write because he had no idea if anyone could write. He said I should write anyway, and said he lay awake all night thinking of words. He died recently, and whenever I'm awake at night and my thoughts turn to contemplating words, I give a nod to his memory.

My first paid short story appeared soon after. I wanted to encapsulate all the frustration in my life. I did it by using a straightforward tale type that I borrowed from Marcel Aymé. He's been one of my favourite writers ever since I could read enough French to enjoy his work. Take an idea and weave it into a story using one single change in the world. Everyday life, twisted. This is how I wrote "Words".

It was published the next year in *Emu: Literary Magazine for Young Australians*. I was paid for it, but it was my first severe edit. An excellent edit, I might add, by, from memory, Catherine Jaggs. She cut out half the story and kept its integrity. This meant I met the guidelines and was paid $10 supplied by the Literature Board of the Australia Council. I like the original which was double the length of the published version you see here. Everyone else prefers the edited version. The bottom line is that there are times when editors know best.

The first story I actually liked that was accepted for publication was to appear in *Aphelion* (and I got a nice letter from Peter McNamara), but it never made it to print until now. This means that it was accepted, but not edited. I wish Aphelion had survived long enough for me to know how Peter McNamara would have edited it.

Cath and I talked about whether she should edit it and we decided that it would be editing it into a modern Gillian's voice and it was written in 1984. Irma Gold helped, and between us we've retained my then-voice rather than made the story into a better one.

It's a shame it's not an Orwellian story, but I failed at a totally available joke because in 1984 I was sublimely serious. It was a different world in 1984. "Mountains of the Mind" is still my favourite story from that time, though it's so much smaller than I remember. It was the short story I hated losing. I may never know how good it was, but I'll always know it was the best story I felt I wrote.

My stories were first lost when I moved from Apple to PC. These were the days when translating between the two was difficult. Many were eaten by a rapacious translation program. A friend tried to save them, so a few survived. I wasn't too worried, because I was Queen of the Backup. My mother had them all. On paper.

When she moved home in 1989, she couldn't find them. 'They're somewhere here,' and we agreed they must be and I didn't really need them. I had entered my gap years and was pursuing public service and social justice with equal enthusiasm. I had a regular income! I had dates! I had no reason to pursue lost dreams or missing stories. This isn't quite true. I just didn't like to push other people to find what was obviously only valuable to myself. The self-image was improving, but it was still a problem. The world around me was far more interested in me writing policy papers and running workshops than me doing what I cared about most. I gave up on the lost stories and put my writing career on hold.

Last year, some of the tales magically appeared. They'd been in a box under the house with a whole lot of other papers, and Mum found them when she moved again. The box contained quite a few of the missing tales.

Between ten and fifteen stories are gone forever. Since the box contained "Mountains of the Mind" I wasn't too worried. I'm still not too worried. It contained my best and my near-worst and they're both in this volume. This means that you should not be too worried either.

Before the Lost Stories came "The Performance". It was not science fiction in any way. I've always loved plays and I wanted to celebrate them. I wrote it for the first competition I entered.

I don't enter competitions, as a rule, except when I have a specific reason. Later I looked into how they affirm certain aspects of culture (as I've said recently on the interwebz, I have odd hobbies), but back then, I needed to find out if Leon Bach was right or if my aunt was right. I wanted to challenge the "I'm not good enough".

So this competition was a test. Regularly I test my self-assumptions about all kinds of things—this is how I manage to get out of holes I dig for myself.

I was in the final years of my undergraduate degree and had to argue if I wanted something. "Breakaway" was never sent for publication because it was very much an articulation of those arguments, but in fictional form. Postgraduate scholarships would help my family understand that I wanted to be an historian, I thought, so the pressure was on with my degree. A prize would help them accept my fiction as worth something. And if I was in international intervarsity debating and got to the grand final, maybe the family would turn up and cheer me on. I did all this: I didn't get the cheers. I did get general support, however, when I got first-class honours, the thesis prize, and the Victorian Ministry of the Arts Award for the short story.

My parents came to see me get my writing award, but for the rest of it, I was on my own. Back then this was pretty much my life as normal. My family is wonderful, but complicated. It added to the feeling that, maybe, I just shouldn't be doing these things. But I had my evidence. I could fight my assumptions with evidence. I was brought up in a very sciencey family and evidence was critical.

What added to the sense that I really didn't earn the writing prize was another piece of evidence: the way the newspaper copyedited the story. They made changes without checking with authors. Because the original typed version is lost, I don't know what's been changed anymore. I do know that I hated all the changes but one. A lot of it was punctuation, but some were words. There was one definite grammatical error added. I've changed the two bits I remember back to what they ought to have remained and left the rest.

That eighteen months that were so successful but had so few feelings of success attached to it are perfectly symbolised by a prize-winning story that was changed without permission. It also taught me that respectful editors, copyeditors and typesetters are worth their weight in gold, and it reinforced my underlying sense that I needed to write. It also helped me realise that my background gave me very little information about what I should do, and that I might be going about it all wrong. This took me a long time to admit, because it meant accepting that life might never be easy or straightforward. This is the world of the Australian Jewish female intellectual who does edgy things. I'm still discovering which judgements are about me and my work, and which are explanations to me that I don't fit and that I should back down.

"The Performance", then, was one of the factors that led to the big gap in my short story writing.

Part One of the collection is everything until the gap years (until 1985 or thereabouts) and Part Two is everything from the moment my life in Canberra caught fire. At that point I damned the ashes, and proceeded to do what I cared about, not what everyone pushed me into. I learned that I was going to be pushed over cliffs on a regular basis. If I'm going to go over cliffs, I decided, I might as well learn to fly.

Before I get to that rediscovery, I get to tell you about how I gave up everything for a very stupid reason. I'll explain the gap years.

I took Serge's advice seriously, which meant I had no guidelines on how to assess my own writing. I was dependent on what other people thought. And, as you have just seen, no one objected to my writing, but they didn't precisely support it, either. The family assessment was that I was at the good end of average at matters academic and fictional and would have to work hard.

I moved to Sydney to do a doctorate because I passed my self-test to follow my dream regardless of my averageness and because research is one of the most fun things round. I was hungry for more, though. My favourite life is full of richness and joy. In Sydney, I made many friends, cooked, danced, and built my first world for a novel. I put a few short stories out there and a couple were published and five more were accepted before the magazines folded. I felt as if I personally handed death to them.

I finished the novel and sent it to Corgi & Bantam. I still have the excited letter from Jean Bedford. She wanted me to consider writing a trilogy. I thought, finally, *Maybe I can write*. She also explained that the Australian office couldn't make decisions on publications. She had sent the novel to both the UK and US offices for approval. Some months later she wrote to me, regretfully, to say that they thought it was not quite suitable for their markets.

I had no way of interpreting this. No writing group. Nothing. Except… what had Serge Liberman said to me? Did he think I was a good writer? He didn't know.

I was not good on the self-confidence front, which I suspect you saw somewhere on the first page of this retrospective where I disbelieved the big prize I'd won for "The Performance". And Serge didn't know. The family said to focus on finishing my doctorate, for I might have trouble doing that. 'Work hard,' I was told. 'Worry about writing later, if you're still interested.' I went into a funk and hid my writing for years.

I still wrote. Of course, I still wrote. I even wrote another novel. It was Tamara Mazzei of Trivium Publishing who called that novel out of the null space it inhabited and edited it in a way that showed me what I could do, and published it and gave me the confidence to write again.

That gap pushed me towards longer narratives and the proportion of novels to short stories changed. The deep void of stories that went nowhere because I hated them, and didn't want anyone to see them, disappeared, because most of those stories were lost. The ones that murdered magazines were also lost. And now some of them are found and in this volume. I'm not sure how to interpret that.

Some of my tales, lost or not lost, were never written for publication. "Whims of the Gods" represents the others in this volume. I was so fractious the day I wrote this tiny tale. So very fractious. I sat down and sarcasmed myself onto the page. I didn't send it to editors. I didn't show it to many people.

Some of the stories lost completely fit into this category. I started writing what I think of as "Daft Tales and True" when I was in first-year university and I was in a debate where we argued the meaning of Gallipoli. I went home and at midnight, I wrote the most appallingly sarcastic retelling of the events that I could. I hated war and I hated turning death into a moment of pride and I hated that I would be stuck with all these interpretations for my whole life because my birthday was on ANZAC Day.

I enjoy being satirical. I tell people it makes me think I'm clever.

Sometimes this side of me erupts into soft little practical jokes. There are two examples of that in this collection. 'Stu's Stew' was first written for a small magazine from Sydney University in the 1980s. When Stuart Barrow was planning *The Gastronomicon*, he set up a submission system and asked for my help to test it. I lightly rewrote the story, including his name instead of the original character's and adding a recipe.

A few weeks later, I mentioned that I planned to write a story for the anthology. He answered, 'I've already accepted your story.'

I said, 'But it's already been published. And this was a joke.'

He scoffed.

The story published here isn't the first version, because his edits were good. It was written when I was twenty-one, however, and edited when I was much older. This is why I gave "Happy Families" the theme of turning twenty-one. I like making connections between my work, for readers who like games and puzzles.

I still can't resist teasing editors. Most of them are very kind about it. Some turn my jokes right round on me and trap me.

Some trap the editor. "Someone's Daughter" looks, on the surface, to be a perfectly normal science fiction story and that's what it was edited as and published as. I only told one of the editors last year exactly what I was doing with it. I shall leave this one as a mystery for you to decipher, but it relates to the story and it relates to female bodies and it was my gift to two male editors (Simon Petrie and Rob Porteous) who were happy for me to use my feminism in fiction.

The jokes, then, aren't new. Nor is my choice of genre. I've always read speculative fiction and I've always reacted to it. "Deus Ex Machina" is a case in point. It has never been a favourite story for me. I wrote it as a private (slightly sarcastic) answer to the science fiction of the time. It's angry about so many assumptions in so very many stories.

Apocalypse was the theme of that minute and it annoyed me. My brain looked at all the tales and said, 'This is not the way the world will end. Let me write the way the world will end.'

So much of what I wrote back then happened inside character's minds, because I've always seen the mind as shaping the reality and I've always wanted to make it clear to the reader that they're not seeing anything clearly, that the world is unreliable. This didn't appeal to editors and "Deus Ex Machina" was commented on in the Peter McNamara episode (for *Aphelion* had looked at and accepted more than one of my stories before it folded without publishing any) as too descriptive. I'd encapsulated the action rather than telling a tale.

I see events this way. It's my inner cultural historian. Events are complex, time-ridden, and so very unlinear. They're like medieval paintings, where every part of a story is linked in a single image, and visible in a single moment. I've learned to unfold this so that other people can live through each moment when they read.

I've never really wanted to live in each moment, though. I want to sit in the middle of the display, immersed in all the time and all the space of the story.

The vast bulk of my writing has been published under my own name. This is due to the short but amusing existence of M.E..

I thought M.E. was a clever pseudonym when I was an undergraduate. I submitted "At the Seaside" to *Yggdrasil* (the magazine of the Melbourne University

Science Fiction Association) and it was published. The editor complained the words were too simple and that sand just wouldn't do that when it met great heat, but all the rest she liked, and it was published unedited. This is the first time I've admitted that M.E. was a pun, and if anyone got it I never heard… and that M.E. is me.

I've used three pseudonyms and one was identified a couple of years ago and I'm not sure anyone noticed. The third is the exciting one. That's why the third is still a secret. Or, not really a secret. Just a bit less obvious. Published somewhere very public. Another mystery to unravel.

I've been told often that most of my work is autobiographical. Even the world-ending stories. One of the first stories published after the null period has been described this way ("A Life—Briefly" in *AntipodeanSF*), over and over. As if it lessens the story, which is an interesting use of "autobiographical" especially when it's not an accurate description.

I'm guilty of calling on my own life for my fiction. Not much is literally from it, however. "Time Is", alone, is pure autobiography. It was never published because, honestly, it's merely a memory I had when I was a student in Toronto. I was twenty-one, on the far side of the world, and I'd just read *On the Beach* as a way of taking myself back to Melbourne. It did. The Melbourne of my childhood. Where everyone died.

I cheered myself up by playing with my own memories. "Time Is" shows what it looks like, then, when I put myself directly in prose. Or this essay shows it. This gives the tools for those who keep trying to guess which parts of the novels are autobiographical. The answer, however, is "None, really". For even if I use events from my life, my actual life is like the moments in the almost-tale.

My life has been spent unpacking these memories and making sense of them. I don't use my novels to unpack these memories, because my novels are fictional. It's that simple.

I still don't much like my short stories, but I'm happy with a couple of my novels. Almost every short story I've written since the null period so gloriously finished has been published. Those that haven't are not published because I've chosen not to publish them. This sounds glamorous, but it actually reflects the small number of stories. There are eighteen published stories altogether, from both generations of my writing.

The second part of this collection is quite different, then, to the first. I'm not the frail soul I used to be. Life is harder now, but I deal with it better and understand the systems better. My new stories have different stories behind them, because of this.

These days I play with themes.

I wrote a group of tales when I was in England and France in the 1980s. The one set in the Royal Albert Hall was actually written there, during a concert. They weren't meant to be clever, just fun. So when Cath and I decided that they'd be a good link between the first half of this volume and the second if I added another to the group, I wondered, *What's the most fun story I've never dreamed of writing?* I reviewed a scholarly analysis of zomromcoms a few years ago and thought, *This*.

Another of my themes is my world-building. The world that most affects my short fiction right now is Alternate History, with the aim of looking (sometimes from a light perspective and sometimes from a tougher vantage point) what continuing prejudice does to cultures. "Wight Asleep" is part of this history.

The rest of that Alternate Earth will emerge when it's ready. This story is merely a teaser, in more ways than one. It's a piece of frivol, but it leads to a project that's not frivolous at all.

This is what I do these days. Most of my fiction is dead serious, even when it's an apparent joke. Life presents us our older selves on a silver platter, and this is who I am. I'm going to be everyone's scary-intelligent ancient woman (I've been called "scary-intelligent" so often I nearly accept it) when I reach old age, and children and cats will think I'm special. Wait, this is me now. I don't know what I'll be later. I do know that the difference between the two parts of this collection is the difference between me-past and me-present.

My stories all still have stories, but the remaining stories for stories belong elsewhere. And who I am and how I change and what life throws at me is a part of all my stories.

Gillian Polack, Canberra
8 March 2018

Acknowledgements

This volume has a long history and a short one. Some of the stories were published and some lost. Some date back to the 1980s and some were written this year. There are so many people who have participated in my short story journey. I can't list everyone, but I can thank them all. Publishers, editors, readers and, above all, friends, going back to when I was still a teenager (barely) helped me begin this journey and enabled me to reach this point. Thank you. Above all, thanks to Cath Brinkley and the discussion about Helen Leonard that made this volume happen.

Some of you are reflected in the stories. I've not used your real names in my tales, for you need the possibility of denial. I don't put real people into my fiction, anyhow. My then-dentist helped with the dental story, for instance, (which was written because I was missing my father) but he is quite a different person!

All historical errors are probably quite intentional and part of a bad joke. I need to thank my historian and archaeology friends for reading specific stories and making sure that I wasn't being an idiot unless I intended to be. They're very patient with the fiction side of me.

The editors of all these stories played critical roles in them reaching the world. In fact, there are so very many writers and editors I need to thank, starting with Leon Bach and Serge Liberman and including the Sydney University French Department (in the 1980s) and the Canberra Speculative Fiction Guild, Book View Café, and many others. The social side of my life brings me to short stories, which means that my friends are part of my writing whether they read my short stories or not. Writers including Judith Tarr, Sherwood Smith, Janeen Webb, Donna Maree Hanson and Elizabeth Chadwick have given me confidence and support when I needed it most.

For each of the previously published stories, a thousand times thank you to:

"The Performance" in *Journal*, Short Story Supplement, 1 February 1982.

"Stu's Stew", first published in an untitled annual student journal from the University of Sydney, 1986. This version published in *The CSFG Gastronomicon*, ed. Stuart Barrow, CSfG Publishing, 2005.

"Summer Job" was first published as "A New Life" in *Kivun*, ed. Leon Bach, 1981, pp. 29–30.

"Words" in *Emu: Literary Magazine for Young Australians*, ed. Catherine Jaggs and Evelyn Tsitas, vol. 2, no. 3, no. 6, Spring/Summer 1985.

"Happy Faces for Happy Families" in *Encounters*, ed. Donna Maree Hanson and Maxine McArthur, CSFG Publishing, 2004.

"'Someone's Daughter" in *Next*, eds Simon Petrie and Robert Porteous, CSfG Publishing, 2013.

"My Life—Briefly" in *AntipodeanSF*, no. 74, 2004.

"Impractical Magic" in *Andromeda Spaceways Inflight Magazine*, ed. Sally Beasley, no. 17, February 2005.

"Being Other" was published in broadsheet form for a Conflux (Canberra Science Fiction Convention) showbag by the Canberra Speculative Fiction Guild, 2012.

"Passport" in *In Bad Dreams 2*, ed. Sharyn Lilley, Eneit Press, 2009.

"Horrible Historians" in *Subterranean Magazine*, ed. John Scalzi, Fall, 2006.

Printed in Great Britain
by Amazon

44796667R00185